Cabo Storm

By Robert Wisehart

First Print Edition
ISBN: 978-0-9894044-9-5
Copyright © 2014 by Robert Wisehart

Published by Black Kettle Books, LLC.
All Rights Reserved

Also by Robert Wisehart

Ethan Cruickshank novels:

Cabo Revenge
Cabo
Cabo Sunset

Sam Houston historical novels:

Born for the Storm
The Lion at Bay
The Rising

Chapter One

I was risking skin cancer hanging out by the pool when my cell phone burbled a call.

"Cruickshank," I said.

"Is this Ethan Cruickshank?"

The voice was male, smooth, and not one I had heard before. I didn't recognize the number either.

"It depends."

"It depends? It depends on what?"

"It depends on what you want. It's always possible that I'm not me. Even if I am I'm probably not in anyway."

"Is this the way you always do business?"

"Are we doing business?"

"All right, why don't we start over?" The voice was more patient than it probably should have been, given that I was such a wise guy for no good reason. "My name is Alton Sterling. I'm trying to reach a private investigator named Ethan Cruickshank at the suggestion of a friend of his in Southern California; Edward Heenan, who is, I believe, better known as Big Eddie."

Big Eddie Heenan *was* a friend, a Southern California skip tracer whose wealth was less a product of his successful business than his way of playing financial markets the way Yo Yo Ma plays the cello. We had worked together a few times, including one tricky operation a while back in Cabo San Lucas, where I lived. I owed it to Big Eddie to at least listen to Alton Sterling.

"OK, I'm me. And even better, I'm in. What do you want, Alton Sterling?"

"I'm an attorney in the Los Angeles area, Century City, to be precise. I'm also the personal representative for Rio LeDoux. I'm sure you've heard of her."

The name rang a faint bell, but not enough to mean anything. And I didn't like the assumption that, of course, I recognized his client, whoever it was. I have found that if you let somebody play it arrogant from the start, chances are they will stay that way and your relationship will not flourish. Besides, I was arrogant enough for both of us.

"I'm sorry, what was the name?"

"Rio LeDoux, the actress."

Now that my memory was properly jogged I recalled that she was, in fact, an actress. She starred in a long-running popular sit-com that I never watched, something about sharing an apartment in the big city surrounded by the usual lovable eccentrics. When that ended, she started making movies, mostly frothy romantic comedies. I never saw those either. I had the impression that Rio LeDoux was in no danger of winning an Oscar.

"Rio?" I asked. "Really?"

"According to her parents, she was conceived in Rio de Janeiro."

"Good thing it wasn't Hoboken."

"Mister Cruikshank, do you enjoy yanking my chain?" Sterling asked, finally letting his exasperation show.

"If I stop, will you tell me what you want?"

"We would like to employ you."

"You do know that I live in Cabo San Lucas, right? Way down at the tip of the Baja Peninsula? Not in the United States?"

"That's one reason Heenan suggested that I contact you," he said. "We're in Cabo now. We're shooting a two hundred million dollar movie here. Or maybe you haven't heard about that either?"

I *had* heard about it, though I was short of details. The locals were practically busting their buttons with pride.

Cabo San Lucas more or less got on the map in the early 1950s, when Hollywood types like John Wayne, Phil Harris, Desi Arnaz and Bing Crosby started coming down from Southern California for some of the best sport fishing in the world. It was hard to get to in those days, mostly by private plane. There wasn't much there either. The Hollywood guys wound up building their own little primitive hotel where they could fish, hang out, drink, play cards and be manly. Once the Mexican government built a decent highway that ran the length of the Baja Peninsula down to Cabo the rest of the world caught on to the possibilities. Cruise ships started coming here and the spotlight triggered a lot of development over the last twenty-five years; resort hotels, time shares, restaurants, time shares, golf courses, time shares, upscale shopping, and, of course, time shares, although the area still retained enough of its old funkiness to appeal to me. Cabo was not Cancun or Cozumel. Good. The fishing was still great, too. It hadn't been fished out like so many other places. I didn't indulge in it myself, but I understood the appeal.

Lately the closest Cabo got to show business were the Hollywood swells that came down for a little sunbaked rest and relaxation. Movies, or parts of movies, were shot here occasionally, but it had been a while.

As I understood it, this movie was a whiz-bang affair that somehow combined science-fiction with swords and sandals, all of it to be larded with nifty 3D special effects never seen by the human eye. Supposedly Cabo had the right mix of water and sand the story needed, not to mention cheap labor the moviemakers needed. Plus, it was close to Southern California. Anybody who got homesick or had to go back for business or personal reasons could get there in a couple of hours on a direct flight to Los Angeles. The eager Mexican government gave the filmmakers a bunch of rousing financial breaks, too.

"You want to employ me to do what?" I finally asked after a too-long silence.

"I would really prefer to discuss it in person," Sterling replied. "It will give you a chance to meet Rio, too. Can you come to our place?"

"Let me guess," I said. "You're staying at the Rock."

"The what?"

"*La Roca*, it means the Rock. They call it The Fabulous Roca."

"How did you know that?" he asked, amazed at my acumen. "It's supposed to be secret. A lot of the people in the movie are staying here. If word gets out we'll be besieged by fans and paparazzi."

Besieged? I thought he was overdramatizing. Self-importance will do that.

"I'm sure word is already out," I explained. "The fact that celebs like to stay at the Rock is about as secret as the faces on Mount Rushmore."

After declaring that I was just as peculiar as Big Eddie said I was, we agreed to meet at the Rock in a couple of hours, which left me plenty of time to ponder just what the hell I was doing.

Chapter Two

I thought about researching Rio LeDoux and Alton Sterling on the Internet, but decided that I would rather get a face-to-face first impression.

As a rule, I like to keep my professional Internet use to a minimum. At first, like everybody else I thought that the Internet was the greatest thing since cold beer. But just because it's on the Internet doesn't make it true and it's getting worse all the time. Any nincompoop can put anything out there and usually does. The Internet also leaves a trail. If there are legal complications, I like having righteous deniability. Sometimes it's necessary, but only sometimes.

And why was I meeting with Rio LeDoux and Alton Sterling at all? Although I took a case from time to time, I didn't need the money. I lived well in Cabo, with a nice house and pool set above the beach not far outside of Cabo San Lucas. The house had a spectacular view of the famous Cabo arch, one of the best-known landmarks in the world. I played tennis a lot and worked out regularly, so I was in good shape.

What I didn't seem to have was ambition, or drive, or whatever it was that wasn't there. Ever since my wife, Dina, died in a scuba diving accident, I felt like I was living at half speed. The word listless probably described it best.

To work my way out of it, I tried everything from women to traveling to drinking too much, sometimes all at once. Nothing much changed except for a recently discovered fondness for Jameson's Irish whiskey. The few cases I took did re-energize me, but only temporarily. Once they ended I was back where I started. I knew that I should work more but the hard part was always the first step; saying yes to potential clients. Most of the time, I turned them down before they even had a chance to finish the pitch. I just didn't want to be bothered. My life was too solitary and I knew it. I needed direction but didn't know which way to go or how to get started. I was drifting and didn't give a damn. I desperately missed Dina, but she was never coming back.

But I was committed to this one, at least to a meeting. I decided not to go armed. I was about to meet a well-heeled client at the most secure resort in Los Cabos, the collective name for Cabo San Lucas, San Jose del Cabo, and all points in between. Unless I intended to respond to lackluster valet service with gunfire, I wouldn't need a weapon. Don't tell me I'm not decisive. With that momentous decision out of the way, I dressed in a light blue long-sleeved shirt with epaulets, the sleeves rolled up on my forearms, khaki pants and black loafers.

After a fifteen-minute drive, I turned off the highway connecting San Lucas with San Jose onto the palm-tree lined road leading to the resort, with the verdant rolling green of a well-manicured golf course flanking both sides. At times like this it was hard to believe this part of the world was all desert, or used to be.

With all the celebrities that stay there, by resort standards security is tight at The Rock. It wasn't Fort Knox, but strangers couldn't just stroll in and act like they belonged without being politely confronted eventually. If they didn't belong there the politely part stopped. Sterling cleared me in advance so getting past the bored guard at the gate was not a problem. He checked my ID and that was it. I drove up the gently winding road to the lobby, where I let one of the eager young men in dark pants and white shirts take my '65 Mustang convertible away, accompanied by the usual covetous stares. It was Arcadian blue with white top and white leather interior. The 289 cubic inch engine had what they used to call a four-on-the-floor manual transmission. I acquired it a few years back when a client didn't have enough money to pay me and I accepted the Mustang instead. It was ridiculous how much I loved the damn thing.

The Rock didn't have rooms; it had "pods," unattached suites of varying sizes ranging from studio to four bedrooms, each one with its own private ocean view, swimming pool and Jacuzzi. Every pod came with its own butler-valet-concierge, too. It was just one guy, but still, not a bad perk. Your wish was his command. The resort also featured two world-class Pat Dye-designed golf courses, a dozen lighted tennis courts, a highly regarded salon, three restaurants that the Michelin guide loved, a night club, its own fishing fleet, a runway for anyone who came in on a private plane to avoid the *hoi polloi* and long lines at the airport, a massive hi-tech workout facility that was always full of beautiful people glorying in their spandex and appreciating themselves in the mirrored walls, and a fleet of electric carts so the residents wouldn't have to walk anywhere, especially to go work out, which always seemed weird to me. You couldn't get in The Rock for less than two thousand a night and that probably got you a little space in a dumpster.

    The only real downside was the paparazzi. Sterling was right about that. Except at the entrance where they tended to congregate - a guard kept them off the grounds - you could not see them, but they were always there, looking for famous faces to bother. With enough successful sneaking around, maybe they'd score a shot of a topless actress or model, a hot young couple doing the horizontal hula, somebody having an affair with somebody they shouldn't be having an affair with, or anything else they could sell to print and internet sleazoids around the world.

    I had to admit that the paparazzi had imagination and were hard to discourage. Sometimes they were known to perch offshore with jet skis and telephoto lenses, until they were run off by either the local cops or resort security. In theory, the ocean belonged to everybody. In the real world, nobody mentioned that to the management at The Rock. From time to time, particularly aggressive specimen might scuba in from somewhere down the beach or a nearby boat and lurk in the shallows, waiting to strike. At least once a year, to gain access one tried dressing like he worked there, but that never lasted long.

    One time, a couple of enterprising lads even rented a two-man submarine to get close to the resort undetected. It actually worked for a couple of days until they ran the little sub into the sandy bottom and couldn't get off. I was surprised that The Rock didn't have a destroyer on hand so it could lay on a few depth charges.

    The resort's open-air lobby was set on a peninsula that jutted out into the blue water, with competing views of emerald golf course on one side and dramatic ocean on the other. As I walked through, I saw the head of security coming my way. His name was Danny Lieber, a retired Los Angeles Police Department captain who made a lot more money at the Rock, where he probably had more manpower and better equipment. Lieber's dark hair was cut military close and he looked like he hadn't gained an ounce since his four-year hitch with the Marines before joining the LAPD. He wore a blue blazer with the gold resort logo on the pocket, a white polo shirt, and light-gray trousers. The slight bulge under his left arm indicated a firearm as an accessory.

We bumped fists. "What's up, EC?" Lieber was the only person I had ever known who called me that. I never bothered to ask why. I've been called worse.

This was not an accidental meeting. Lieber knew I was coming because Sterling cleared it with security. He was good at what he did and paid attention to details. When a private detective entered his domain, he wanted to know why.

"Maybe a client," I explained. "A check-each-other-out meeting."

"Oh, yeah? Who?"

He already knew the answer, but I gave it to him anyway.

"An actress named Rio LeDoux. Her rep called and wants to meet, a guy named Sterling, Alton Sterling."

Lieber rolled his eyes. "Good luck, EC. You're gonna need it."

I realized there was another reason why he intercepted me in the lobby: I had been warned. Call it professional courtesy.

"LeDoux or Sterling?" I asked.

"LeDoux, big time. Sterling seems okay, for a lawyer."

Business concluded, he asked, "You hear about the hurricane?"

"I know there's one out there. It's that time of year, though maybe a bit early."

"Looks like it's headed our way."

"They usually veer off. Cabo hasn't been hit in a long time. It's still pretty far away, too."

Lieber nodded. "Yeah, but maybe we're due. I dunno, I got a feelin' about this one."

Chapter Three

I caught a ride on one of the electric carts the Rock used to transport residents around the complex and was taken down a winding asphalt path to Neptune – all the pods had names instead of numbers – where I rapped on the door.

A young hotel employee - probably the butler-valet-concierge that came with the place - let me in and showed me to a leather reclining chair in the living room. I had barely touched cushion when a man entered the room through the sliding glass doors from the patio. He was a couple of inches under my six feet, two inches, with distinguished silver hair cut to perfection. The shoes were Italian leather, worn with no socks. The slacks were dark gray, with a pink pullover shirt. Very GQ casual. He was slim and looked like he was in shape. His upper arms were thick enough to show that he worked out, but not so defined that he was showy about it. It was hard to tell his age, one of those people who could be anywhere from mid-forties to mid-sixties.

We shook hands and introduced ourselves. His handshake was dry and firm, without overdoing it. Glancing out to the shaded patio, I saw a round table with an open briefcase stuffed with papers and a laptop computer beside it.

After dismissing the hotel employee, Sterling motioned for me to sit.

"Would you like something to drink?" he asked.

"No, thanks."

He took his place in an identical chair directly across from me, about six feet away.

"Rio's at wardrobe, getting some fitting done for the movie. She'll be along soon. I thought we might take the time to go over what we want before you two meet."

I nodded my assent.

"What we need is security for Rio while she's here," he explained. "I'm sure you can appreciate that anyone in our position is vulnerable to all kinds of things. It's a constant concern wherever we go."

"How long will she be here?"

"The shooting schedule is six weeks, though we don't start for a few days. The movie business being what it is, I think two months is about right, maybe even longer. These things tend to expand."

"What about you?" I asked. "Will you be here the whole time?"

He shook his head. "I'll probably stay another few days then I'll be back and forth. I *will* be here a lot, if that's what you're asking."

Something didn't make sense.

"Mister Sterling, I'm sure that the studio could provide additional security, or would if you asked. And the police chief here is a good man. He probably could help you out, too. Why the need for somebody like me? That tells me something out of the ordinary is going on, or might be."

Sterling smiled approvingly and laced his fingers in front of his chin.

"That's very impressive. You *are* good. And by the way, please call me Alton. The fact is that we would rather not request extra studio security. I'm afraid that Rio's had certain, ah, issues in the past. At this point, we'd rather not appear to be excessively difficult."

I noticed that he said "appear" to be difficult, as opposed to actually difficult, which she probably was if Lieber's warning was on target. And it was interesting how he often used the words "we" and "us."

"What sort of 'issues' in the past?" I asked.

Sterling looked out the sliding glass door at the beach and ocean beyond before he answered.

"It's no secret that Rio's been in and out of rehab several times. Her struggle with drugs and alcohol is ... ongoing. And some of her past acquaintances have been, shall we say, unsavory. In a way, she is quite naive. As I said, at this point we would rather not call attention to her, um, vulnerability, so we would prefer to quietly hire private security."

Sterling chose his words so carefully it was like he was sifting through diamonds.

"Regarding local police protection, while chief Valencia did impress me as a capable man, he admitted that the movie shooting here was taxing his already overextended department and he has no extra manpower to give us. He also recommended that I contact you, by the way. He didn't know that I had already spoken to Heenan. Between the two of them, that's quite a good testimonial. Most impressive."

I tried to look modest while he continued.

"As to your final point, your instincts are sound. In addition to the unknown, there is a specific possibility we want to guard against. Rio was briefly married years ago. By briefly, I mean for two weeks and they weren't together for even that long. It was a quickie Las Vegas wedding when she was at her most vulnerable, one that she instantly regretted. They'd known each other for less than twenty-four hours. She wasn't at her, ah, best during that period. Given the brevity of their marriage he received a more than generous settlement when they divorced. Unfortunately, he occasionally reappears in her life, a very bad influence. I believe that he might even want her help professionally. At one point, he fancied a Hollywood career for himself. We believe that he broke into her home in the Hollywood Hills a few weeks ago and we've had reports that he may come here, or perhaps he's already here. It's imperative that we keep him away from her. I can't emphasize that enough. The man is nothing but trouble, but he seems to have a strange hold over Rio. She has a lifelong soft spot for the bad boys of the world; unfortunate, because she could do so much better."

"If he's harassing her and broke into her house why not just have him arrested or get a restraining order?" I asked.

From what Sterling already said I knew the answer, but I wanted to hear it anyway. Getting people to talk is a big part of what I do.

"We don't need any more bad publicity," he replied. "That man would love the attention of an arrest, anything to get his name in the public eye. But with Rio's past excesses, it could ruin her, especially if

11

there was a trial of some kind with all the media attention that would come with it. Even in our business, despite what people think you only get so many chances before the downward spiral starts. As I said, this movie is important to her, vitally important."

Before we could go any further, the door slammed behind me and a voice screeched, "OK, where the fuck is this fucking private eye who's supposed to be so fucking good?"

Rio LeDoux was in the building.

Chapter Four

Sterling and I got to our feet as he made the introductions.

"Rio, this is Ethan Cruickshank, the private detective that came so highly recommended."

Without a glance in my direction, she headed to the well-stocked bar with a determined stride.

"So find out what he costs and hire him, for Christ's sake. Do your job. I've got other problems. From what I saw today, fucking wardrobe might as well dress me in a fucking mu-mu. Jesus! I'm gonna look like a fucking tank."

She planted herself behind the bar, reached down behind it and found a bottle of Patron tequila. She poured a shot, downed it in one gulp, poured another shot and downed it, too.

Rio LeDoux was about five feet nine inches tall, with glossy shoulder-length hair that was either black or dark brown, depending how the light hit it. Like most actresses and models, she was too skinny for my taste, although she was buxom as hell, which she showed off nicely in the crop-top she wore with white shorts. The crop top also revealed abs as toned as they were tanned. Her dark eyes were flashing and aggressive and she had a strong, almost masculine, jaw. Put it all together and she was more striking than beautiful, but striking she certainly was. There was no obvious face work that I could see.

Tearing her attention away from the tequila, she looked me over like I was on the auction block, nodded toward Sterling and said, "He tell you what we want."

I nodded back.

"He ask what you're gonna fucking cost?"

I probably heard that word every day of my life, but there was something about the way she said it that sounded ridiculous. It was as if she was trying to show the world how tough she was, but didn't know how to do it other than to say variations of "fuck" a lot.

When I shook my head, she said, "You don't talk much, do you?"

When I still didn't reply, she poured herself another shot to follow up the first two.

"Well, why don't you tell me how much I'm gonna have to pay you to stand around and do nothing?"

"A million dollars," I said.

That stunned her into silence, but not for long.

"What the fuck did you say?"

"I'm sorry, but you waited too long. The price just went up," I replied. "Now it's a billion dollars."

Mouth hanging open, LeDoux turned to Sterling. "What's this dipshit talking about?"

Although he recovered quickly, Sterling looked as flabbergasted as his client. It had probably been a long time since anyone sassed Rio LeDoux.

"I believe Mister Cruickshank is saying that he doesn't want to work for us," he explained.

"What!" She slammed her shot glass down on the bar, expensive tequila sloshing over the side. "Just who the fuck does this asshole think he is?"

With a wave at Sterling, I said, "Alton, you seem like a decent guy with a hard job and I'm sorry that I wasted your time. But I'm even sorrier that I wasted mine."

As I closed the door behind me, I heard a crash on the other side, just about head high. It was the shot glass, no doubt about it. The resort staff would have some cleaning up to do.

Rio LeDoux was a foul-mouthed pain in the ass, but she did have a good arm.

Chapter Five

Recovering the Mustang from the valet, instead of driving home I went to *Gaviota*, the tennis and fitness club I belonged to in Cabo, where I kept a locker with my gear. I needed to sweat the charming Rio LeDoux out of my system.

Ninety minutes later, I was pretty successful. There was nobody around to play tennis with so I worked out, followed by some stretching as I cooled down. When I was younger, the conventional wisdom was that you stretched before you started. Now they say that's a good way to hurt yourself before you've even warmed up and stretching should be done at the end. The next time conventional wisdom changes its fickle mind, it'll have us all stretching in the middle or not stretching at all.

I showered at the club and drove home; where the first order of business was to crack open a cold Negra Modelo. I'd earned it. The second was to call Eddie Heenan from my chair by the pool where I could watch the fishing boats come in at the end of the day.

When Heenan answered, I could tell that he was on the road somewhere, probably in his Corvette, and I was on speaker.

"Hey, Ethan, my man," he said. "What's up?"

"Eddie, I just wanted to thank you for the fabulous career opportunity."

Noting the sarcasm, he said, "You connected with Sterling, didn't you?"

"And the charming Rio LeDoux."

"From your tone, I assume it didn't go well."

"You assume correctly. I'd rather work with a tarantula. How do you know her, anyway?"

"I wouldn't say I really know either one of 'em very well. I own a company that does security work for the studios. I ran into her and Sterling a couple of times."

"You've got *another* company?"

"Sure. Why not? Like they say, you can never be too rich or too thin."

Since Heenan stood six feet, six inches tall and weighed two hundred and forty five pounds of bulging muscle, too thin was out of the question. He probably worked out by lifting his wallet.

"You know, once you get to know her she might not be as bad as she seems at first," he said. "You never can tell."

"Eddie, nobody's as bad as she seems. I'd probably get more money from people who'd pay me to shoot her."

He laughed at that. "I get you, but you gotta understand it's mostly an act. Underneath all the bullshit, she's probably scared to death and trying like hell to keep it together. She doesn't always succeed either."

"Scared of what?"

"Of everything. Her last couple of films didn't do well and she's scared that her career's going down the drain. If the movie they're making down there does good box office, or if she's good in it, it's a game changer for her. She'll get better scripts that'll turn into better movies. So she's under a lot of pressure and that probably scares her, too. She's scared of getting old in a young person's game, especially for women. She's made a lot of money but she's spent even more and she's scared of going broke. She wouldn't be the first. She's scared of going back to rehab for the umpteenth time but she's scared to stop taking anything she can get her hands on. Her fuck you attitude drives good people away, but she's scared of being alone. Up here at least, she surrounds herself with parasites that enjoy the ride. For all I know, she's probably scared of the dark."

"I thought you didn't know her very well?"

"I don't. I just described about half the people in Hollywood. From her reputation, she's in that half."

"Sterling seemed okay, assuming there's such a thing in his line of work," I said. "Why doesn't he do something? Maybe get her to a shrink."

Shrinks were something I knew about, having spent some time in their company. My parents were killed – beaten to death – when I was a kid. I was in the room when it happened. I knew that psychiatry doesn't always work. But I also knew that sometimes it does, or at least it helps.

"My guess is that even if he tried he's just a hired hand and she's not known for listening to reason," he said. "I'm not sure how much longer he'll be in the business anyway. I've heard that he's cutting down his client list, probably slowing down like everyone does eventually. He's been at it for a long time. Anybody else would have dumped her by now, but he seems to have genuine affection for her. God knows why. I hear she treats him like crap, until she needs him to get her out of trouble."

"Well, she's gonna be somebody else's problem while she's down here."

"Fair enough. I just thought you might be interested. You've had worse clients. I mean, it's about time you got back in business."

I saw it now. Heenan was trying to do me the favor, not Sterling and LeDoux. "I'm doing fine, Eddie."

"No, you're not and we both know it. Everybody who knows you knows it. You won't like to hear it but I'll say it anyway: Dina wouldn't like the way you've been since she died. You owe it to her to pull it together."

"Go to hell, Eddie."

"No doubt about it," he said, just before I ended the conversation.

Chapter Six

Two days later, Sterling called again. This time he didn't sound as smooth.

"He's here," Sterling said urgently. "You've got to help us."

"Who's where?" I asked.

"Rio's ex-husband. He actually showed up at my door. Rio's staying one pod over from me and he must have thought this was her place. She's registered under another name. I opened the door before I knew who it was. I tried to stop him but he pushed me away and marched through the place shouting, 'Where is she? Where is she? What have you done with her?' It was as if he thought I was in the wrong and he wanted to save her. When he finally figured out that she wasn't here, he left."

"Why are you calling me? Call resort security or call the police."

"I told you why. And I don't know where Rio is either. She's not in her place and she doesn't answer her cell. Under normal circumstances, it hasn't been long enough to worry, but with him around …."

There was an awkward pause while he waited for me to say something. When I didn't, he broke the silence.

"Please, *please*, help us! There's nobody else around here I can call!"

Oh, hell, I thought. What else is there to do?

"OK, I'll be over in a few minutes. Clear me with security so they don't hold me up. And unless it's Rio, don't open the door to anybody but me."

Since I didn't know what I'd be facing, unlike my first visit I decided to go armed. I keep two guns at different places in the house and another under the dashboard of the Mustang, but none of them are good carry weapons. I have a gun safe where I keep my weapons behind a concealed door in the closet of the master bedroom. I am no collector, but over the years I've acquired a lot of firepower, some of it taken from people who did not wish me well.

Today I decided to take the Springfield XD-S nine-millimeter. With a polymer frame and seven-round clip, it's small and light, but still has good stopping power. The flat, narrow profile made it an easy carry in the holster at the small of my back, too. With my shirt untucked, only an expert could tell that I was armed.

Driving like a maniac, I made it to *La Roca* in record time. Seeing my distinctive blue convertible, the same gate guard I encountered earlier waved me through. Instead of valet parking, I wheeled the car into the underground garage. If I had to leave quickly for any reason, I didn't want to wait for somebody to bring the car around. I raced upstairs to the lobby and got a ride on one of the resorts' electric carts, but not all the way to Sterling's pod. I wanted to approach on foot.

I eased around to the back and came in from the beach, so that anyone watching the front wouldn't see me coming. As I approached the sliding glass door, taking care to come up from one side, I saw Sterling in the living room pacing back and forth. When I rapped on the glass, he practically jumped out of his expensive shoes.

"Any word?" I asked as he let me in.

He shook his head. "Nothing."

"Is the ex-husband staying here?"

"I have no idea," he replied. "I didn't see a cart, or anything, when he left."

That didn't help. He could have come on foot like I did.

"What's his name?"

"Troy, Troy Kearns."

"Troy? You're kidding?"

Sterling ran his fingers through his hair like he needed something to do with his hands. Under the circumstances, I didn't blame him for not seeing the humor. The controlled man I'd met a couple of days ago was on the verge of losing it.

"His real name is Elmer. He's had acting and writing ambitions over the years and thinks the name Troy makes him stand out."

"Describe him."

Elmer "Troy" Kearns was five nine or ten and weighed around two hundred pounds. According to Sterling, he was a fairly serious body builder, bulky across the chest and shoulders. His blonde hair was cut close.

OK, I thought, a short-haired fire plug should be easy to spot.

But first I made a call. His name was Anthony, at least that's what he said. I didn't know his last name, or even where he was. He liked it that way. He was a tech wiz who could do anything with a computer. Nothing was too obscure that he couldn't find it given enough time, including people. He also was great at answering questions, any questions. I didn't know much about him except that he was an albino who was extraordinarily sensitive to light, which meant that he didn't, or couldn't, get out much. That probably explained why he did what he did. At least he had a good reason to be a nerd. In addition to his per task fee, I kept him on a modest monthly retainer so that he would respond quickly when I needed him. I hadn't contacted him in more than a year, but I never got around to canceling the retainer. This was one of those times when the Internet might be my friend.

"Cruickshank! It's been a long time since I've seen that number come up."

There was just the slightest hint of an accent, one that could come from almost anywhere except the Deep South. The voice was neither young nor old.

"Anthony, I need something,"

"I rather figured that."

"Rather?" British maybe? With every call, I tried to find a bit more about the mysterious Anthony. I had the feeling that he enjoyed playing the game by dropping hints here and there. The problem was that I didn't know if the hints were the real thing, or a way to send me off the trail.

"The name is Kearns." I spelled it out. "His real first name is Elmer, but he goes by Troy."

"Troy? Seriously?"

"Yeah, I know. At least it's not Rock or Tab. He lives in the Los Angeles area but he's here in Cabo San Lucas and I need to know where he's staying. He might be at a place called *La Roca*, otherwise known as The Fabulous Roca."

"How soon?"

"Now would be good."

"Give me a few minutes."

Two minutes and fifteen seconds later, he called back.

"That was fast, even for you," I said.

"I must say that *La Roca* has very good security when it comes to defending against the usual."

"But you're not the usual."

"I certainly hope not. Your boy Troy is staying at *La Roca*. He's registered as Elmer Kearns, which indicates that's still his legal name. He checked in yesterday, last night at 10:12, actually. He's in Nautilus, whatever that means. He flew into the airport at San Jose del Cabo on American Airlines out of Los Angeles."

"Is he by himself?"

"The room, or whatever it is, is registered for one. I can cross check the passenger list on that flight against the list of people staying at the resort, if that will help. But if he has someone with him, they could be in another room, or perhaps staying elsewhere. *La Roca* is an expensive place and Kearns' card is not far from its maximum. If he stays there more than a night or two, it will be interesting to see what happens when he checks out and can't pay the bill."

It would be good to know if Kearns had help, but I decided against waiting for the information.

"Why don't you check that out and I'll call when I can," I said. "I've got to get moving."

"All right," he agreed. "And Cruickshank?"

"Yeah."

"Don't worry about the hurricane, at least not this one."

"Not you, too," I said. "Everybody's talking about the hurricane. They're obsessed by it. Chances are it won't even hit Cabo. It'll probably veer off like most of them do."

"I quite agree," he said. "That's my point. It almost certainly will do exactly that. According to the model I developed for a client, the chance that it will hit Los Cabos is less than ten percent and decreasing everyday."

"That's good news."

"However, there is another problem," he said.

"What's that?"

"There is an eighty four percent chance that you will be hit by a hurricane this season," he said.

"Eighty four percent?"

"Exactly, according to the model."

"Anthony, I gotta go," I said. "But next time try to be a little more precise.

Chapter Seven

Like all guests, Sterling was given a map of *La Roca* when he checked in. It showed that Nautilus was down the beach a couple of hundred yards. He wanted to come with me but I didn't like the idea.

"You need to be here in case Rio comes back." I tactfully didn't mention that he was so jumpy that he'd probably drive me crazy.

"And you don't want me tagging along and getting in the way if anything serious happens," he said.

I shrugged a reply. "Yeah, something like that. This is what I do."

I went out the slider, past the pool and Jacuzzi and headed down to the beach, which was at least a hundred yards deep. It was pretty empty, with a few *palapas* scattered here and there and a handful of resort guests gathered under the shade of the *palapas* in lounge chairs, wanting to be as close to the ocean as possible. The waves were pounding in and sending spray twenty feet in the air. White jacketed cabana boys, or whatever they were called, tended to the guests' needs, which mostly involved food and drink, trudging back and forth between the resort and the beach.

I didn't want to be noticed or remembered, so I ambled along, trying to look like I was going nowhere in particular, but still moving as fast as an amble would take me. Following the map, when I reckoned I was just short of Nautilus, I turned into the resort grounds.

I hopped over a stucco wall and cut across the back of the pod next to Nautilus, which made a good looking redhead lounging by her private pool lunge for a towel to cover herself, giving me a dirty look at the same time. I would have leered, but I was in a hurry.

I approached Nautilus the same way I approached Sterling's Neptune, from the rear toward the patio. As I neared the sliding glass door, I saw Kearns standing in his living room, talking on his cell phone. Sterling was right. The man did serious weight work. His muscle shirt was packed and bulging.

I saw something else, too, a pair of red sandals next to the white leather couch in the living room. Just a couple of days ago, I'd seen red sandals on Rio LeDoux's feet.

Busy with his telephone, Kearns eyes widened when he saw me a few seconds after I saw him. He tossed the cell phone on a chair and opened the slider.

"Who the hell are you?"

I kept moving, wanting to get as close as I could to see inside. At the same time, I held up one hand in a peace gesture; a man apologizing for the interruption.

"Sorry, but this resort is sure confusing, especially coming in from the beach," I explained. "I'm looking for the Odysseus pod, but I got lost. You wouldn't happen to have a map of the place, would you?"

I had no idea if there was such a thing as the Odysseus pod, but I figured Kearns didn't know either. With my eyes moving from Kearns to the living room and back again, other than the red sandals I didn't see anything suspicious. If Kearns had help, a roommate, or an actress, there was no sign of it.

"Whaddya lookin' at?" Kearns demanded, noticing my divided attention. "Tell you what, why don't you get lost. I might even help you on your way."

He moved toward me in his best tough-guy mode, doing everything but flex. I shuffled back to give myself some working room and shuffled right into the Jacuzzi set almost flush with the patio floor.

I fell like I was in slow motion. The water was hot but fortunately not deep. Kearns was so surprised at my sudden stumblebum act that he stepped back and dropped his hands, which gave me the opening to come out of the water like a tidal wave. If I didn't make a comeback soon this could be really embarrassing.

Kearns seemed confused about what to do and settled on trying to kick me in the head when I came out of the Jacuzzi. Dumb move.

Unless you're a martial arts expert, a kick is not very efficient. The arc of the foot is too long.

Which I proved when I blocked the kick, caught his foot in my hands, held his leg parallel to the ground and swept his other leg out from under him with my foot. He hit the tile hard on his tailbone, the wind knocked out of him with a loud "Uhh!" He rolled over on his side and I left him lying in the fetal position, gasping and trying to get his breath back. He wasn't going anywhere for a while, muscles and all. Getting the wind knocked out of you like that is the next best thing to temporary paralysis.

I stepped around the helpless Kearns and went through the open slider into the living room. Seeing nothing of interest other than the sandals, I moved on to the master bedroom.

And there was Rio LeDoux, barefoot but fully clothed in mid-thigh shorts and a sleeveless blouse that buttoned down the front. She was lying face up on a bed that was big enough for five people, eyes wide open and stoned out of her bazoo, mumbling and gesturing to her inner self.

After a quick check of the patio to confirm that Kearns still was in no condition to be troublesome, I got LeDoux out of bed and on her feet. It wasn't easy. She wasn't dead weight as much as she seemed to be going several directions at once.

"OK, darlin'," I said, mostly to myself. "It's time to get the hell out of here."

We passed Kearns on the way out. He was still where I put him; on the ground and struggling to get his wind back as his angry eyes followed us. Not wanting to take chances, I settled LeDoux in a lounge chair and kicked Kearns hard in the ribs to keep him down a while longer.

The best way to get LeDoux back to her place was to go the way I came. She wasn't walking as much as stumbling, like she might fall down any second. I put my arm around her waist to hold her up, with my other hand on her forearm closest to me for balance. With luck, we looked like lovers on a beach stroll. Every so often we'd stop to admire the ocean while I eased the cramp in my arm.

The journey was complicated because I had to look over my shoulder to make sure Kearns wasn't after us. Fortunately, there was no sign of him. Maybe I broke one of his ribs when I kicked him? The thought made me happy.

When I finally got LeDoux back into Sterling's pod, his relief was evident on his face until he saw her condition.

"What's wrong?" he asked, going frantic on me. "What did that bastard do to her?"

"She's stoned out of her mind," I said. "Other than that, she seems fine. Did she have any drugs with her? It might be good to know what she took."

"I can't be sure," he admitted. "But I don't think she had anything. I know she didn't bring any into country."

"Probably old Troy had a stash," I said.

I had Sterling call the resort desk and demand that he and LeDoux be immediately moved to other quarters. Fortunately, the Rock is used to guests who are as whimsical as they are wealthy and the change was agreed to with no questions asked. Within three minutes of Sterling's call, enough resort personnel showed up to transport a family of five across the country. The move didn't take long. We were on our way in less than ten minutes from the time I made the call. The new pods weren't far away, but Kearns didn't know that. I kept an eye out during the move, but didn't see anyone watching.

Once LeDoux and Sterling were settled, I told Sterling that I had to go home and pick up a few things, including a change of clothes, but I'd be back in an hour, or so.

"Don't answer the door for anybody but me and draw the curtains on the back slider," I instructed. "Make sure it's locked and keep it that way. If you see Kearns outside, or even think he's out there, call hotel security. Don't try to be brave and don't talk to him, not one word. Just make the call."

I left LeDoux sprawled across Sterling's bed, still mumbling and gesturing.

"It doesn't look like she'll be any trouble for a while," I said.

I called for an electric cart and it took me to the underground garage, where Danny Lieber was leaning on my Mustang, arms crossed across his chest.

"EC," he nodded.

"Danny," I nodded back.

He looked me up and down.

"You're all wet. Forget your bathing suit?"

"Some days there's nothing like a nice refreshing dip," I said.

Lieber shook his head. "You need to know something, and I wanted to tell you face to face. You get one pass with me and *this* is that pass. We had a complaint from a young lady who said a guy who sounds a lot like you violated her privacy, not to mention get a good look at her knockers. Then one of my people saw you walking down the beach with an obviously drunk or stoned Rio LeDoux. When he took a look at where you came from he found that the guy in Nautilus had been knocked around, though he wouldn't say who did it or why."

"Gosh, I hope he's not badly hurt," I said.

"He'll live," Lieber said, grimacing at my phony concern. "Nothing hurt but his pride."

Lieber was still leaning on my car, but despite the casual stance it was clear that he meant business.

"So maybe you're working for LeDoux and Sterling. OK, you landed a nice rich client, good for you. To tell you the truth, I don't really give a shit. The thing is you can't act like a cowboy here. If there's a problem, see me about it. I know you well enough to know that you're gonna do what you're gonna do. But the next time you get out of line on my turf I'm comin' down on you like the wrath of a very pissed off god. Understand? What happened today slides, but that's the only break you're gonna get."

I understood his point of view. He was doing his job. I hate it when that happens.

"I have to come back here, Danny," I said. "And I will."

"I figured you might," Lieber said. "I'm not barring you from the grounds. Not yet. But you've been warned. You've had all the leeway you're gonna get."

Lieber got off the hood of my car. I got in and drove away. Lieber watched me go.

I guess I had a new client after all.

Chapter Eight

I was so distracted that I was most of the way home before I realized that my Springfield wasn't in its holster.

Thinking back, I realized it probably fell out when I tumbled into the Jacuzzi. The embarrassment of the fall still burned a little. It probably explained the extra oomph I put into the kick I gave Kearns.

If the gun wasn't in the Jacuzzi, it was right beside it where we had our scuffle. If Kearns didn't have a weapon before, he probably had one now. Good move, Cruickshank. Now you're arming the bad guys.

When I got home, I got out of my wet clothes and took a shower to wash off the Jacuzzi water. I dressed, packed a bag good for several nights, just in case, and re-armed myself, this time with a Ruger LCP .380. It's light, even with its six-round magazine, and small enough that it's comfortable in an ankle holster. The range was limited to about twenty-five yards, but I didn't plan to shoot elephants at five hundred yards.

I called Anthony to see if he had any more information.

"I cross checked the names on Kearns' flight from LAX with the *La Roca* register, but nothing matched, except Kearns, of course," he said. "The other passengers are scattered all over, from Cabo San Lucas to San Jose del Cabo and in between, including a couple up the coast in Todos Santos. Three of them didn't show up anywhere, so I assume they're staying with someone, or they're natives."

"Kearns was alone when I saw him, though that doesn't mean anything," I said.

"Yes, Ethan, do remember that he could have help, it just isn't staying at *La Roca*," he said. "For what it's worth, the man doesn't seem to have any kind of criminal record either. Maybe he's new at being a baddie?"

Anthony chuckled and it turned into a cough, one that sounded like a smoker's cough. Okay, say he's British and maybe he smokes, I thought.

"By the way, you brought some excitement into the lives of the *La Roca* staff," he said. "There was a flurry of texts and emails where your name was prominently mentioned and not in a complimentary way. The head of security there, a man named Daniel Lieber, is not in your fan club."

Thinking out loud, I said, "What would be the point of Kearns having help if it's somewhere else?"

I had the answer to my own question right away. Even having someone north in Todos Santos would make sense. The movie was shooting up the coast in that direction. If somebody was looking, like Anthony, for instance, it made Kearns' help harder to find, too. Although for all I knew, he was flying solo.

"Mine not to reason why, old boy," Anthony chuckled again. "All this detecting is your department. It seems positively exhausting to me ... wait a minute! Well, well, well, whatever happened when you, ah, *saw* Kearns, as you put it, must have scared him, or had some effect."

"Why do you say that?"

"Because he checked out a couple of minutes ago. I just saw it come up."

"Got any idea where he's headed?"

"It's a bit too soon, even for me. It will show up sooner or later unless he's staying with someone in a private home. There's no record that he rented a car when he arrived in Cabo either."

"So he got out of *La Roca* as soon as his location was known. Either somebody picked him up, or he took a taxi or shared a van. If it's a taxi or van it means he didn't go far. I wonder if he went to the airport?"

"I thought of that. I'm checking now." I heard Anthony's keyboard clicking in the background. "It doesn't look like he's on any flight out of Los Cabos today. Shall I continue to look? Sooner or later, he'll show up. Everyone does. Even people who go off the grid, as they say, aren't really out of sight. They just think they are. It shouldn't be too hard to crack *La Roca*'s security cameras, too. Perhaps that will show us *how* he left the resort. If he used a taxi or van and I can see the name of the company, it will be easy to find out where it took him."

I had a feeling that hadn't come on me since the last time I worked with Anthony. Sometimes the ease with which he did what he did was a little creepy. I knew that genuine privacy was an increasingly rare commodity in today's world. But working with him brought it home the way nothing else did.

Not that it stopped me from using him, of course.

"Keep looking," I said. "Let me know if you find anything interesting."

"Ethan, to me, it's all interesting. And do get ready for that hurricane, old boy."

Old boy? Yes, English, I thought. I bet Anthony is English.

Or not.

Chapter Nine

The next several days involved plenty of nothing, unless you count boredom as something.

There was no sign of Troy Kearns. It turned out that the security camera at *La Roca* that might have told us something wasn't working. Knowing Danny Lieber, it wouldn't stay that way long.

I dutifully tagged along with Rio LeDoux. For a couple of days she was uncharacteristically subdued after her bout with what she confessed were too many peyote buttons before I snatched her away from her ex-husband, an adventure that she claimed not to remember at all, thanks to being stoned at the time.

I don't know what LeDoux told Sterling, if anything, but she wouldn't tell me any more about what happened with Kearns, or how it happened. Yes, her silence was irritating, but it was her call. It was my job to keep it from happening again, not to rehash history. Given what Sterling told me about the relationship, it was my guess that she went with him willingly. Maybe it was as simple as the bad boy attraction, like Sterling said. I'd known it to happen. I had no doubt that she took the peyote willingly, too. That could complicate the situation if Kearns showed up again. LeDoux was an adult, at least in years. Legally, I couldn't keep her from doing anything. Even if I could, I probably wouldn't. I'm a detective, not a nanny, though there have been times when it amounted to the same thing. Whatever might happen had to be against her will before I could prevent it.

The movie's working title was *The Watchers*, although everybody involved with it seemed sure that would change once the marketing people went to work. It had something to do with space aliens in ancient Egypt. Yes, the old *Chariots of the Gods* baloney lived again.

LeDoux's character seemed to be based more or less on Cleopatra, but without the inconvenient presence of Julius Caesar or Marc Anthony. There was no sign of the asp.

Back when we lived in Southern California, I had a few clients in the movie business and I was roughly familiar with the process of making one. Some think that it's glamorous, but I found that hanging around on the set and watching the magic happen was as glamorous as watching ice melt.

Every morning, a black Lexus SUV picked up LeDoux at *La Roca* and took her to the beach location about ten miles north on the coast from Cabo San Lucas, which was set up to play Alexandria, Egypt. The moviemakers planned to shoot interiors and blue screen work later at a huge old warehouse in Cabo that was recently converted to several state-of-the-art sound stages, basically a whole new movie studio named Baja Productions. The computer-generated stuff would be done in the United States at a facility in the San Francisco Bay area. With the shiny new studio, subsidized almost entirely by the Mexican government, Cabo hoped to lure more movie production. It was good for the local economy and added gloss to Cabo's reputation, as the parade of politicians and VIPs who visited the set emphasized.

When LeDoux was on location but not needed for a scene, she spent almost all of her time in her trailer, a beast that was bigger than Nebraska and better furnished. The director and the movie's stars all had one, all of them the same size down to the inch. I learned that such details were a standard part of movie contracts, called a 'favored nations clause.' If so and so had something, then all the movie's hot shots got it, too. LeDoux did not deign to invite me inside.

I was given a copy of the script and the shooting schedule so that I could anticipate where LeDoux might be at any given time, although I soon found out that the information was meaningless because the movie was already behind schedule. After only three days of shooting, it somehow managed to be two days behind. In my boredom, I'd already eaten too much of the catered food, especially the chocolate donuts with coconut sprinkles. My future on this job was looking fat.

I was familiar with LeDoux's leading man, Johnny Miles. I'd seen several of his movies and liked most of them. In person, he was handsome and friendly and seemed, well, stupid, not to mention a lot shorter than I thought. Another ideal dashed.

Miles didn't seem to care for his co-star. Being Rio LeDoux, she returned the favor with interest. From what I could see, they had all the chemistry of a doormat and a bowling ball. It did not look promising for the rousing sex scene they'd be shooting later on a closed set and shown in all of its 3-D glory.

In the middle of the third day, after one supposedly simple scene with LeDoux and Miles that required so many takes I stopped caring, she stormed off the set to her trailer, slamming the door behind her to emphasize that she was a touch cranky.

While the crew set up for the next scene, the director, a tall skinny guy named Niles Odermeyer, who had a couple of Oscar nominations on his resume, made the pilgrimage to LeDoux's trailer. Although he had the look of a man who was about to meet his mother-in-law at the airport, he managed to charm his way through LeDoux's barrage of closed-door invective and get inside so the conversation could be more or less private, which to me meant that he might be a better actor than his actors.

Lurking nearby, through the trailer's thin walls I heard LeDoux rant about how doing a scene with her co-star was "like working with a loaf of bread."

Odermeyer calmed her down by agreeing that Miles wasn't giving her much, though maybe the loaf of bread thing was a little harsh. After offering the observation that the actor liked to "work his way" into a role, meaning that he *would* get better, maybe, Odermeyer assured her that the slow and lousy work they'd done so far wasn't her fault. He promised that he'd have a talk with the loaf and see if he could get Miles engaged in what he was doing, which seemed like a reasonable request in return for the actor's fifteen million dollar paycheck, plus a percentage of the gross.

After forty-five minutes of verbal abuse, wails, hand-holding and many promises, as the director left the trailer, weirdly dressed in a safari hat, khaki shorts, and a black turtleneck, the first turtleneck I'd ever seen in Cabo, he looked like he'd gone fifteen rounds with a giant squid.

Seeing me still lurking, he sidled over and introduced himself. His eyes were bloodshot and his handshake was all bones.

"You're Rio's security, aren't you?" he asked. "The guy who rescued her from her ex."

I was a little surprised that he'd heard about it, although for all I knew the episode was plastered all over the northern hemisphere. In some ways, I was out of touch in Cabo. In most ways, I liked being out of touch.

Still, with me, Sterling, LeDoux, Kearns, and Lieber and his security team all involved in one way or another, it was naïve to think that what happened could be kept quiet. I acknowledged that I was all of those things and much more. Curious about who might have leaked, when I observed that the presence of the ex-husband and LeDoux's rescue was not supposed to be public information, the director only laughed.

"Rio's not very good at keeping anything to herself. She's better than CNN. And if you're looking for suspicious characters you might want to keep an eye on me. There's a good chance I might shoot her before this is over."

When I laughed, Odermeyer laughed, too, his Adam's apple bobbing in his skinny throat.

"I'm just kidding, I think," he said over his shoulder as he walked back to the set to commit more show business. "But check back in a couple of weeks."

And so it went. Every morning I followed LeDoux from *La Roca* to the set. I always drove the Mustang. If anything happened, I wanted my own wheels. Nothing slows down a pursuit like having to bum a ride. Leaving Cabo San Lucas through its not very appealing back side of light industry and strip malls, far away from all the tourist attractions, we drove north along the coast, always taking the same road because there was no other choice.

Once we got out of town, for most of the drive the ocean was at a distance on the left, with cactus, scrub and brown rolling hills on the right. Getting to the location required a half-mile drive off the highway down a rutted dirt road to the beach.

The road out of Cabo was in good shape but not much used the further out of the city you were, with notable exception of delivery trucks running between Cabo and La Paz, the biggest city in southern Baja, and tourists headed to the art colony of Todos Santos. I figured that if somebody, like, say, her ex-husband, wanted to grab LeDoux and knew what they were doing, the road would be a good place to try it. Run the limo off the asphalt and pull her out of it before anybody came along.

It would be my job to thwart such a thing, although by now I was half-convinced that the worst threat might come from her co-worker.

Chapter Ten

LeDoux solved the problem with her leading man in her own unique way.

The day after her blow up with Odermeyer, LeDoux's work for the day was finished shortly after noon. But instead of heading back to *La Roca* as she usually did, she retreated to her trailer.

It was mine not to reason why, so I waited. About thirty minutes later, along came Johnny Miles. Dressed in civilian clothes, capped teeth agleam, and with a friendly nod in my direction, he stepped up to LeDoux's door, knocked an obviously pre-arranged signal, and stepped inside with a big smile when the door opened.

One hour and three donuts later, Miles stepped out of the trailer wearing a different smile, a satisfied one. After offering me a salacious wink, he went on his way with a jaunty stride.

As a professional investigator, I knew a clue when I saw one.

Thirty minutes after that, out popped LeDoux, with a curt nod in my direction to indicate that she was through for the day. As usual, I escorted her to the SUV, followed her back to the Rock in the Mustang, and rode with her in the electric cart to her pod.

Probably sensing my curiosity about the change in her relationship with a guy she recently compared to a loaf of bread, she turned in the doorway to defiantly face me, one hand on her hip and a challenge in her every molecule.

"Yeah, I fucked him stupid, if that's what you're wondering," she said in her usual too-aggressive way. "From where you were standing, you probably heard the whole thing with Odermeyer the other day, right?"

When I nodded that I had, indeed, heard, she said, "I'll probably have to fuck that meathead again, too. But now, when we're working and I look in his eyes, at least there's something there."

She sighed a sigh that was heavy with disgust. Or maybe she was just tired?

"And you know what? That dumbass is no better at screwing than he is at acting."

The defiant attitude radiated from her like plutonium, as if she expected me to disapprove of what she was doing. If so, she was doomed to disappointment. I'd been on enough movie sets to know that it happened all the time. Shooting a movie is like living under a bell jar. What happens there doesn't count in the real world.

Besides, I didn't particularly care.

"You probably think I'm a slut, don't you?" she said, entering her living room.

"Not really," I said, pulling the door shut. "I mean, what the hell? Anything for art."

Chapter Eleven

Valencia, the Cabo San Lucas police chief, came by the following day.

We'd known each other for a while, although our introduction was a little rough: He had me handcuffed and ready to take up residence in a Mexican jail. And all I did was shoot somebody. Fortunately, the relationship improved with time.

I spotted him strolling in my direction from the parking area off the road from the highway, seeming casual but taking in everything around him the way he always did.

"I see that they hired you despite my advice," he said.

I took a sip of the coffee I was drinking in an effort to stay awake.

"They said you recommended me."

Valencia shook his head mournfully. "The language barrier is a terrible thing. So much misunderstanding. How is it going so far?"

"Boring as hell."

"Boring is good," he said.

"Coffee's over there." I motioned to a big stainless steel urn on a table underneath a canopy that was set up to provide shade on the beach. Soft drinks, lemonade and munchies were available, too. I'd sworn off the munchies, a vow that I'd probably break in about an hour.

Valencia drank more coffee than anyone I've ever known. If I put down as much as he did, I've have the heebie-jeebies all day every day, but it didn't seem to bother him at all.

He walked over to the canopy, filled a white plastic cup with coffee, added his usual tonnage cream and sugar, and walked back. His precision of movement made the simple act of drawing coffee look like an art form.

Valencia probably was the best cop in Mexico and one of the best I've known anywhere. He attended the FBI academy in Quantico and worked for Interpol in Europe before joining the Cabo police. The illegitimate son of a powerful but shady character I knew only as the general, who was assassinated not long ago on the mainland, Valencia was under constant pressure to move up to bigger things, but liked it where he was and refused to budge. The Mexican higher ups respected that and mostly left him alone. Cabo is an important tourist attraction and Valencia had a way of doing his job without being heavy handed, although he was known to clash with authority from time to time. I had been involved in a couple of those clashes. He was middling height and slim, but deceptively strong, with a black mustache that matched his hair. He was expert in several martial arts and probably could kill with a Popsicle stick.

"So where is the actress you are protecting so diligently?" he asked.

"She's sulking in her trailer," I said, pointing my head at LeDoux's giant home away from home. "That's what she does when she's not in a scene. They won't need her for a couple of hours, though the way this thing is going they might not need her at all today, or this year."

Valencia sipped his coffee and I sipped mine. He had two uniformed men out on the highway where the dirt road branched off to keep the civilians out and a couple more floating around the periphery of the set. I assumed that there were others out of uniform, too. His dark eyes were always on the move, checking out his men and looking for holes in the coverage.

"Any trouble in town with the movie people?" I asked.

"Not yet," he said, taking another sip of coffee. "If we have any, and I am sure we will, it will come later, when the crew starts to get bored and begins drinking too much."

"Why does your department even have this duty?" I asked. "We're well outside of Cabo San Lucas. It must put a real strain on your resources."

"It seems that the government has a misguided opinion of my capabilities," he replied. "That and we're closest and there is no one else. Mexico City wanted to send federal people here, but I don't need uniformed men in riot gear strutting around my town with their automatic weapons and machismo on full display. For one thing, it seems to make you *gringos* uneasy."

Another sip of coffee. "I told Mexico City that we could handle it with the resources we have, but it *is* a strain. I have every man in the department working twelve-hour shifts seven days a week. Some of the men are even sleeping in the jail so that they will be immediately available, if necessary."

He looked at me over the rim of his coffee cup.

"And how are you doing?"

"Well enough," I said. "I guard like hell, though so far there isn't much to guard against, with one exception."

"I heard about your confrontation with the ex-husband," he said.

"Join the crowd," I said. "It seems that everybody has."

"Any sign of him?"

"Not so far. Maybe I scared him and he gave up?"

"Do you really believe that? You're not that scary."

"Thanks. I do have to assume he's out there somewhere. It'd be dumb not to."

"And your client?"

"She's a head case who's as arrogant as she is insecure. So far she's only driving the director nuts. At least that's all I know about. But give her time. She'll spread it around."

"If you need any help, let me know."

"How? You're stretched as far as it goes now."

"I didn't say that I'd help. I just said let me know. Are you ready for the hurricane?"

I looked out at the calm ocean and bright blue sky. It wasn't even very humid, which Cabo often is this time of year, and the breeze was light and lovely. It was like living in a postcard.

"Not you, too, with the hurricane business," I groaned.

"Yes," he said. "Me, too. Something is coming. You can bet on it."

Valencia tossed the remaining coffee to one side, flipped his paper cup into a big green trashcan, and with a curt nod headed back the way he came.

I realized that checking on his men was only part of it. He was checking on me, too.

Chapter Twelve

I was still worried about security at The Rock.

With all the movie people, plus the usual well-heeled tourists, the resort was at full capacity, so there wasn't any place to put me so I could stick as close to LeDoux as I liked. When Lieber suggested that I sleep in her extra bedroom, Sterling rejected the idea like I had anthrax.

Most upscale resorts and hotels routinely hold a few places open for unexpected VIPs, but I was assured that this time that wasn't an option. There really was no room at the inn.

Sterling wasn't staying at the Rock either. Given his travels between Cabo and Los Angeles, with the high demand the resort couldn't hold his pod when he wasn't there. The Rock had too many repeat customers to take care of. When Sterling was in town, he wound up staying at the almost-as-posh *El Grande Cabo*, a couple of miles away.

When I visited Lieber's tiny office off the resort lobby and explained my concern about security, he said that he'd been thinking about it, too, and had an idea.

"It's something we've been working on for a while and this just might be the time to give it a ride," he said. "That is, if LeDoux is willing to move again."

When he gave me the broad strokes, I thought she might go for it, depending on how artfully he sold it. There was nothing like it anywhere that I knew of and she'd certainly like the idea of getting the special treatment.

LeDoux's first response was to complain, of course, but Sterling talked her into at least taking a look.

"Just let them show it to you, Rio," he said. "Believe me, you've never seen anything like it." It was an interesting comment considering that he hadn't seen Lieber's idea in action either, even though he was selling like Willy Loman.

With the rest of us hanging on for dear life, Lieber barreled the electric cart down the asphalt path to a two story pod. Carrying a brown leather brief case in one hand, he slipped the card key into the lock and we walked in.

Lieber turned on the lights. Before LeDoux could say anything, he beat her to it.

"Other than having two floors it doesn't look any different, does it?"

He placed the leather case on the living room bar, opened it, and pulled out a cuff bracelet. It was beautiful workmanship - silver with an Aztec design inlaid with three turquoise stones - but what was the point? I couldn't believe that Lieber was trying to entice LeDoux with an expensive present.

He handed the cuff bracelet to the skeptical actress and told her to slip it on her left wrist if she was right handed, or on the right if she was left handed.

Once she had it on her left wrist, he said, "Okay, press that turquoise on the far right."

"What the fuck is this?" she asked, pressing the stone.

As soon as she did, the storm shutters that provided shade around the patio closed with a crash. At the same time, more shutters fell at every window in the unit and a sheet of polished steel came down at the sliding glass door leading to the patio. The transformation was so swift and loud that it stunned everybody but Lieber, who expected it.

"Okay, that's phase one," he said, turning on a light from a wall switch so we could see each other. The storm shutters blocked out all sunlight.

"You see a bad guy coming, or anything you don't like, just press that and you might as well be locked in a safe. Even if he gets to the patio, he's trapped. He can't get in and he can't get out. It sets off an alarm at our office, too. If my men aren't here in less than thirty seconds, I will fire whoever is on duty."

LeDoux looked at the bracelet on her wrist like it just performed magic. For once, she had nothing to say.

"You said something about phase one?" I asked.

"Okay, Miss LeDoux, now hit that second turquoise, the one in the middle."

We heard doors slam followed by loud clicking sounds all through the pod.

"That just closed and locked every inside door. You run into any room – any bathroom, any bedroom – hit that button and you're safe. Underneath the wood, the doors are reinforced steel. Nobody's getting through unless they're carrying a rocket launcher."

"I almost hesitate to ask about the third button," I said. "What does it do, repel boarders?"

"That one may be the most interesting of all," Lieber said. "You've noticed that, unlike all but a few of the pods at The Rock, this one has two floors; living room, dining room, kitchen, bedroom and bathroom downstairs and two bedrooms and two bathrooms upstairs."

When we all nodded like school children, he said, "Okay, now, follow me."

He led us to an area under the stairs, a place that most two-story townhomes use as storage. Most of them have such a small doorway that you practically have to bend double to get through. But with this one, even at my height I could walk in without stooping.

Lieber opened the door. "Miss LeDoux, please go in. When you're inside, press that third turquoise."

She walked in, pressed the turquoise, and the door slammed shut and locked.

"You okay in there?" he asked.

"Yeah, some kind of recessed lighting came on when the door closed," she replied, her voice muffled by the closed door. "I can feel air conditioning, too. There's even a sink and toilet. It's a lot bigger than it looked from outside."

"Okay, hit the button again and come on out."

When she emerged, Lieber explained.

"What you have here is what some people refer to as a panic room, a refuge of last resort, just in case. Again, the door is reinforced so nobody else can get in once you're inside."

He removed the bracelet from LeDoux's wrist. "So we have three lines of defense that cannot be penetrated, not that we'll need them all, of course. We probably won't even need one. Believe me, you could not possibly be more secure and still retain your privacy."

Lieber spoke directly to the actress. "So how about it? Are you willing to move in? It's a bigger place than what you're in now. We've been working on this project for more than a year and you would be the first to use it."

I could tell that LeDoux was tickled by the whole thing, especially being the first. The look on her face said, "All of this for little old me?"

Lieber went back to his leather case on the bar so that he had his back to us. He fiddled with the contents, and then turned around.

"You have three choices. One is the cuff. The second is this necklace." He held up his hand and let an expensive silver chain dangle from his fingers. Attached was a pendant with the same Aztec design as the cuff, including the three turquoise buttons. "And this is number three." In his other hand was what appeared to be a switchblade style automatic car key, the kind of thing you see everyday. But instead of symbols for the doors and trunk, it displayed the by now familiar turquoise buttons.

"It's your choice, of course, but I recommend the cuff," he explained. "For most people, it's easier to get to. You can hold it out in front of you when you press the button, meaning that you can see what else is going on at the same time. You'll have to pull the necklace away from your body to see what you're doing and you'll have to take the key out of your pocket, unless you try to activate it by feel. But in that case, you'll risk pressing the wrong button."

Lieber gently replaced the cuff on LeDoux's wrist, a tender gesture that was almost like a caress.

"We had the best jewelry designer in Mexico create the style we wanted. No one will know that it's anything other than it seems to be, a lovely piece of jewelry. It looks beautiful on you, just as you look beautiful with it."

By now Lieber could have sold her bridges in Brooklyn and home sites in the Everglades. He had a deal.

Chapter Thirteen

Sometimes you just get lucky.

I was driving LeDoux to a production meeting in town. After the meeting, she was scheduled to make a personal appearance at the Chamber of Commerce to show a happy face to the movers and shakers of Cabo San Lucas, part of the movie company's public relations effort. We were stopped at a stoplight when I saw Kearns on the sidewalk just ahead of us.

Without telling LeDoux that I spotted her ex-husband because I didn't want her to get squirrely on me, I wheeled the Mustang into a no parking zone next to a *mercado*.

"I just saw something I've got to check out," I said, interrupting her in mid-curse, which was her version of asking why we stopped. I slipped the key out of the ignition and into my pocket. "You stay here. I don't know how long I'll be. If the police come and want you to move, tell 'em who you are and where we were going. Tell 'em the car died and I went to get help. Whatever happens, don't go anywhere until I get back. If there's trouble, scream and you'll have more help than you can handle."

Before she could protest, or, more likely, complain, I was out of the car and on Kearns' track. The Mustang was well known to the Cabo police and with a movie star in it I figured I had a good shot at not getting towed.

I caught up with Kearns and crossed the street to follow him from the other side. It was late-afternoon and tourists were out in force seeking bargains so it was an easy tail. A tough tail is when the street is empty and you don't know the turf. He didn't seem to be in a hurry as he casually strolled down *Lazaro Cardenas* into the center of town before turning into the arched entryway of the Hotel Cortez.

The family-owned Hotel Cortez was one of the oldest hotels in Cabo, probably dating back to the 1950s. Until recently, it was showing its age a little – actually, more than a little - but its age was part of its charm. A million dollar-plus facelift on the old place did wonders, at least from the outside. While its Spanish Colonial architecture was as rustic as the rooms were basic, it was one of the best deals in Cabo. You could get a room at the Cortez for around sixty dollars a night and a suite for less than a hundred. Although you didn't get an ocean view, it had a decent swimming pool and bar-restaurant. A lot of people liked it for its convenient location. Step out on the street and you were right in the middle of town. It was especially popular with budget-minded families and young couples, plus dedicated fishermen who didn't care about the usual tourist attractions.

My immediate problem was that there were only two ways in: the front entrance that Kearns took through the lobby and the hotel parking lot in the rear, which required a code to open the rolling metal gate. I didn't want to go through the lobby because I didn't know where Kearns was and didn't want to risk being seen.

And then sometimes you get really lucky.

My phone chirped. It was Anthony.

"I found your man," he said.

"I found him, too," I said.

When I explained what happened, Anthony confirmed that Kearns was registered at the Cortez. He even had the room number.

It turned out that when Anthony couldn't find Kearns as quickly as he thought he should, he took it as a challenge. After a little research, he came up with a list of everyone who checked into a Cabo San Lucas hotel the day that Kearns checked out of The Rock. Then he told the computer to throw out women along with anyone who arrived in Cabo that day. Although the list was long, cutting it down apparently it wasn't as difficult as it seemed to a layman like me.

"I was disappointed that Kearns' name still didn't appear," Anthony said. "Then I fed his driver's license photo into some software that recognizes faces while tapping into all kinds of data bases, including hotels and their lobby security cameras. Not every hotel has a camera, but most do these days. That's how I found him, although he's working with a forged passport, driver's license, and credit card. He has a rental car, too, a white Volkswagen Jetta. Not bad, wouldn't you say? What's the saying, 'They can run, but they can't hide?'"

Anthony sounded pleased with himself. I didn't blame him.

"What's the name he's using?" I asked.

"John Childress from Davenport, Iowa." Anthony gave me the Jetta's license tag number, too.

That was good, I thought, very good. A pro created Kearns' fake ID. Davenport, Iowa, is a place everybody knows but no one has been to. It wasn't very likely that you'd run into someone from there, but the familiar name was comforting. You just have to trust somebody from Davenport, Iowa.

"Thanks, Anthony. You're worth every dollar that I under pay you. Let me know about anything significant, but especially if he checks out of the hotel."

"Will do, Ethan. Be well, and be careful."

Now what? I had an idea. A plan was taking shape.

I went down the side street to the parking lot in back of the hotel. It was exactly as I remembered; a rolling chain-driven metal barrier that denied access to anyone who didn't have the security code. I loitered on the street for a while, waiting for someone to either leave the parking lot or come in. After fifteen minutes, a Nissan Sentra with a family of four stopped in front of the barrier while Dad reached through the window and punched in the code. The barrier slowly rattled open, the Nissan passed through, and just as the barrier was about to shut I eased through, too.

I hunkered down behind an SUV while the Nissan disgorged the family and its luggage. It was like watching a circus clown car unload. How much more stuff could there be? Once Mom, Dad, two kids, and several tons of luggage were in the hotel and safely out of sight, I found Kearns' white Jetta just to confirm what Anthony told me, and then waited for another vehicle to come or go so I could get out.

A deeply tanned older man wearing baggy shorts and a sleeveless t-shirt, who I bet was in Cabo for some serious fishing, came out of the hotel, got into his Toyota Corolla, drove up to the barrier, waited for it to open and drove away, with me happily escaping behind him. You needed the security code to get in, but not to get out.

On the way back to the Mustang, I popped into a little *mercado* and bought a pre-paid disposable cell phone with cash, making it impossible to trace. The plan was in motion.

Chapter Fourteen

Good news: the Mustang was where I left it.

Bad news: Rio LeDoux wasn't in it.

If she had to leave for some reason, it would be much too responsible for the actress to go on to the production meeting. There was no chance of that at all. In retrospect, I wasn't surprised that she drifted away. I don't know why I expected her to act like a responsible adult and do what I told her.

I figured that she'd gotten bored and went looking for something that pleased her, a good guess since looking for something that pleased her was what she seemed to do almost all the time. LeDoux didn't know Cabo, so I didn't think she'd go far. She didn't have to anyway. A majority of the bars, restaurants and clubs are within a five or six block square area of where I left the car, including the area around the marina.

So I began looking, up one street and down another, methodically poking my head into everything from upscale clubs – most of them weren't open yet – to hole-in-the-wall bars, with a lot of shops and restaurants, too. The more I looked, the more I fumed.

After about forty minutes, I saw a crowd where there shouldn't be one and approached to see what was going on. It was a tiny outdoor bar with six or seven stools adjacent to a dozen shops that catered to tourists; leather goods, cheap blankets, turquoise, coral and silver jewelry, and lots of bottles of Kaluha, with its distinctive yellow label. It was a great place for people watching; the endless – and sometimes scary – parade of humanity up and down Marina Boulevard.

Only this time the parade, or some of it, had stopped to watch Rio LeDoux.

She was sitting at the middle of the little bar, surrounded by mostly male admirers. One strap of her pullover top had slid down her shoulder. Her tanned legs were crossed at the knees, and her upper body leaned heavily on the battered copper and wood bar, supported by one arm. On the bar in front of her were a shot glass and a half-empty bottle of tequila. I'd been gone for not much more than an hour and if she drank all that tequila alone then she had to be seriously drunk.

Oh, good, I thought. It just keeps getting better and better.

I pushed through the crowd to get to her side, where I was greeted by a slap on the shoulder. She was so drunk she nearly missed me.

"Well, halloo there, big boy." Eyes bleary and limbs rubbery, with a boozy grim she took in the mostly male crowd surrounding her. "Boysh, thish is kind of my bodyguard. I mean, he's kinda guardin' my body, if ya know what I mean." She arched her back to emphasize breasts that stood out like snowplows. "Well, waddaya think, boysh? Is he doin' a good job, or what?"

Judging by the laughter, it was the funniest thing her new friends had ever heard.

"It's time to go, young lady." I took her arm above the elbow and pulled her off the bar stool, catching her with my other arm around her waist before she fell to the floor. "I think you've had five or ten too many."

I was prepared for trouble but to my surprise I didn't feel any, despite the river of alcohol flowing all around us. Any group of people has a character or tone—happy, sad, hostile, confused. With this one, all I felt was confusion.

A hand tentatively touched my shoulder and I turned. He was young, maybe early twenties, maybe even younger. Still more boy than man. His face was burned red from too much sun, which happens a lot to the tourists who come to Cabo from cold places and are determined to get a tan even if it kills them.

"Mister, if you know her maybe you can help explain somethin' to us," he said. "She says she's Rio LeDoux, you know, the movie star, but nobody's sure if we should believe her. I mean, sure she kinda looks like her, but what would somebody like Rio LeDoux be doin' here gettin' drunk like this?"

And that was my way out. It's a strange thing about celebrity. I'd seen it before. People don't believe that celebrities are to be found where the rest of humanity is wont to dwell. They don't believe that celebrities go to the grocery store, the ball game, or the bathroom. A real celebrity doesn't go to the movies, go window shopping, or get drunk among strangers at a small outdoor bar in downtown Cabo San Lucas where you can buy a shot for a couple of bucks. Instead, they do what marvelous things they do in some rarified world that the rest of us can only imagine but never visit.

They didn't believe that she was Rio LeDoux because Rio LeDoux couldn't possibly be here in this place with them, could she?

"Yeah, I know," I said, with a sad shake of my head. "She does that when she has a few too many. I mean, they do look a little alike, I guess, but it's the booze talking. It can be a helluva problem, too. She's gone through some tough times and I feel sorry for her. I think she just wants to be somebody else, somebody famous with a better life that she has. I'm no bodyguard either. I'm just a friend who's been lookin' for her for most of an hour. Her boyfriend and his pals are out lookin', too, and he's really gonna be pissed if he sees her like this. I'd sure like to get her back to the hotel before he does. Would you mind givin' me a hand?'

Sure, it wasn't my best deceit, but it didn't have to be. Most people are nice. Tell them that you have a problem and they'll feel sorry for you. Ask for their help and they'll give it. I was taking advantage of that good nature.

With help from my now solicitous friends, who said they'd even pick up her tab, I got LeDoux wobbling in the direction of the Mustang while she bellowed, "But I *am* fuckin' Rio LeDoux, godammit!"

"From what I've heard, who hasn't?" I muttered.

Chapter Fifteen

By the time we got back to The Rock, LeDoux was passed out in the Mustang's passenger seat and snoring up a storm.

Cars are not permitted on the resort grounds. With the help of an attendant, I laid her out in the back seat of an electric cart, hopped in the front beside the young driver and told him where to go. I found the card key in her pocket, opened the door, carried her inside, and none too gently dumped her on the bed. In her condition, she was about as attractive as a sack of fertilizer. I removed the cuff from her wrist so she wouldn't accidentally shut the place down and unnecessarily alert Lieber's troops.

Then I called Sterling, who was in his room at *El Grande Cabo*. When I explained what happened, he said he'd be right over. True to his word, he was knocking on the door fifteen minutes later.

"How the hell did this happen?" he demanded. "Weren't you supposed to be with her?"

It was a reasonable couple of questions, all things considered.

When I told Sterling how I spotted Kearns, followed him, and LeDoux's temporary escape, he started running his fingers through his well sculpted hair just like he did the first time she went missing.

"Oh, great! That's just what we need! What are we going to do now?"

"I have an idea," I said. "Can you stay here in case she wakes up and wonders what the hell happened?"

He nodded. "Sure. What are you going to do?"

"It's probably better that you don't know," I said, heading out the door.

Chapter Sixteen

One of the more peculiar items in my inventory of firearms was an old Smith & Wesson 38. It's at least fifty years old and looks like something Mike Hammer might have used when he wasn't getting his fedora blocked. I couldn't even remember how I acquired it. I had never used it and, although it was nicked around a little, it still was in good shape. By the time it got to me, the serial number was removed by acid and the weapon was taped so that there wouldn't be any fingerprints, neither of which was characteristic activity of a law abiding citizen.

I'd finally found a use for it.

Late that night, I returned to the Hotel Cortez, after parking the Mustang in the pay lot a few blocks away at the Wyndham. Many tourists, especially young couples and singles, tend to stay out late in Cabo, often gravitating to Cabo Wabo, a place to which I had never been and, with luck, will never go. With sufficient patience, I didn't think I'd have a problem finding a car to follow into the Hotel Cortez parking lot. I could always climb the cinder block wall, but I didn't want to risk being seen.

I waited a half hour, which seems a lot longer when you're standing on a dark side street trying not to look conspicuous. A popular restaurant, *Missiones de Kino*, was in the same block, so I passed the time in the shadows around the corner where I could see the parking lot but not be seen by the diners or street traffic.

Finally my patience was rewarded. A Kia rental rolled in and I rolled in right behind it.

I had checked during my earlier visit in the daylight and saw no security cameras in the parking lot. Kearns' white Jetta hadn't moved, or if it had he parked it in the same place. It took a couple of minutes for me to break into the car, which was slower than I used to be, mostly because

I was out of practice and a little nervous. I hadn't used this particular skill in a while. The usual sense of galloping paranoia coupled with the tingling feeling around the groin when you're doing something sneaky and blatantly illegal was something I never got used to.

Once I got the driver's door open, after a quick glance around to make sure nobody entered the lot from the hotel, I slid the 38 under the driver's seat. I didn't want to do anything too fancy because I wanted it to be easily and quickly found.

This time it was more than an hour before I was able to escape from the parking lot. I didn't want to leave through the lobby because the desk clerk might remember someone headed out this late, especially a single man. Eventually the rolling door clanked open and once the entering car, a Ford SUV, passed I slid through again, walked to the Mustang at the parking lot, paid my expensive fee, and drove home.

The downside of my plan was that I had to get up early the next morning after a night that didn't have enough sleep. I didn't want to wait too long because Kearns had to be in his room for my plan to work the way I wanted it to. I didn't figure him for an early riser, but it was best to make sure, so I rolled out at six.

There was a convenient little restaurant across the street and down the block from the Hotel Cortez that opened early and served a bountiful breakfast. Yawning until I thought my jaw might crack, I planted myself at a table outside where I could see the hotel entrance. I ordered coffee, orange juice, very well done potatoes, and a ham, cheese and mushroom omelet, with a gallon of salsa and a tortilla on the side. After my first cup of coffee, but before the breakfast arrived, I called the hotel on the disposable telephone I bought yesterday.

"*Hola!* Hotel Cortez!"

"I feel awkward doing this," I said, speaking rapidly and breathlessly like I was nervous. "I've stayed at your hotel several times and really like it. But I saw something in the parking lot yesterday that I really should report. I have the feeling I probably should call the police about it, but you've always been so nice that I figured I'd call you first. I don't want to get the hotel in trouble."

The police threat was important to my plan because it would get the hotel personnel moving.

"If you will wait just a moment, *senor*, I will get the manager. Perhaps it is best that you tell him what you have to say."

After a pause, a male voice was on the line.

"How may I help you?"

"There was something I saw yesterday afternoon in the parking lot. I worried all night about it before I decided to call. I don't want to get anybody in trouble, but I really felt that I should report it. At the same time, I don't want to get involved."

"I understand completely, *senor*. Now, if you would please tell me what you saw."

"There was a man in a car, it was a white Jetta, I think. He was sitting in the driver's seat. I saw him reach down – maybe between the seats, but I don't know – and pull up a weapon, a gun, actually. He did something and the thing in the middle of the gun came down and he started loading it."

"A gun, you say?" Now the voice was alarmed. "Are you certain? This is a very serious thing."

"Yes, I'm sure. Like I said, he was loading it. You can understand that I didn't wait around to see what happened next. I just got out of there in a hurry. I thought about it all night and finally decided that someone should know. I mean, we've been coming to Cabo for years and this is the first time I've ever seen anything like it."

"I understand what you are saying, *senor*. Did you get the license plate number, by any chance?"

"Gosh, I'm sorry. I completely forgot. I was in such a hurry to get out of there that I didn't think of it. But it was a Jetta, a white Jetta, and, like I said, it was a rental, from Alamo. I think. I better go now. My wife is waiting. You know how it is."

"*Senor*, I ..."

I ended the call just as my breakfast appeared.

And I waited.

Chapter Seventeen

The way I figured it, the manager would go out to the parking lot in back of the hotel to see if a car fitting the description was parked there. Anyone with a car who registered at the hotel was required to give their tag number to the clerk, so it would be easy to identify who belonged to the Jetta and what room they were in.

Then the manager would return to the front desk, or, more likely, go to his office for privacy. He'd contact the police and tell them about the mysterious caller, adding that there *was* a car fitting that description in the parking lot and it belonged to a guest named John Childress from Davenport, Iowa.

And, the manager would ask, what should he do?

The answer: Do nothing until the *policia* arrived.

Despite what many North Americans think, Mexico has strict gun laws. If you are caught with an unauthorized firearm you can be sent away to an unpleasant place. I get around it by having dispensation from high up in the Mexican government. I'd done a few things that made the Pooh-Bahs in Mexico City like me, or so they claimed, some of which they didn't want generally known. It was like having a get out of jail free card where you didn't have to go to jail in the first place.

Valencia was especially strong in this area. It was one of the ways that he kept Cabo relatively crime free. Given a chance, he probably would come down on Kearns like a falling safe.

I was about halfway through my breakfast when a police car quietly pulled up in front of the hotel, a no parking zone where cabs and airport vans load and unload people and luggage. Out popped Valencia from the passenger's side. The chief's presence surprised me until I remembered how stretched the Cabo police were with the movie in town. He was accompanied by a ridiculously young uniform cop who looked like he might weigh 120 pounds if you included the weapon on his hip. He would not strike terror into the criminal heart.

Valencia entered the hotel with his scrawny underling trailing along like a puppy following a lion.

About fifteen minutes later, just as I was finishing my breakfast, Valencia and his underling came out of the hotel, with a bewildered looking Elmer "Troy" Kearns between them. Old Troy's hair was as mussed as short hair could be. Even from a distance, I could tell that he still wasn't fully awake, rudely rousted out of a sound sleep by unsympathetic police. His hands were cuffed behind his back. The underling carried what appeared to be something heavy and dark in a couple of plastic baggies, handling them very carefully.

Two baggies? Strange.

Valencia carefully eased Kearns into the back seat of the squad car, with the hand on the noggin technique police use to keep the prisoner from conking his head and claiming that the cops abused him. Not that it would have done much good in Mexico, where you are guilty until proven innocent.

It was a typical Valencia operation—quiet, fast and effective. The car left just as quietly as it came, with the chief in the front passenger side, the kiddie cop driving, and Kearns contemplating his fate in the back seat. I resisted the urge to wave.

Ten minutes later, I paid for my breakfast in cash, wanting no record that I was there. On my way to the Mustang, I disposed of my disposable telephone.

Chapter Eighteen

That afternoon, stifling my yawns, I escorted LeDoux to the public relations function she missed the day before, a gathering of Cabo San Lucas' most prosperous and successful men and women. Despite their status, all of them seemed star struck and eager to have their picture taken with the celebrity.

LeDoux was surprisingly good at it, starting with a few words about how she was so pleased to be in Cabo and how much she enjoyed their beautiful city. She even threw in a few phrases in clumsy Spanish, which charmed the hell out of everybody. She showed no signs at all of her alcohol-rough day before.

She was even better at the mix and mingle session afterward, although the three glasses of wine she downed like water probably helped loosen her up. She was a movie star, after all, and used that considerable wattage to great effect. She had a way of making each person she talked to feel like for just a moment there was no one else in the world except the two of them. It had nothing to do with sex. I saw it work on both men and women. For the first time, I saw what a good actress she was, or could be.

I was doubly surprised when Valencia showed up.

"*Hola, jefe*," I said. "I didn't think this was your kind of thing."

He was in full uniform for the occasion, compete with a Glock on his hip, a crease on his trousers that you could shave with, and not a wrinkle on him.

"It certainly isn't 'my thing,' as you say," he said. "I came here to see you."

"I'm flattered. What about?"

Valencia's intense dark eyes bored into mine.

"An odd thing happened early this morning and I thought you should know about it."

"What might that be?"

"We arrested Elmer Kearns."

"Really!" Astonishment showed in my every fiber. "What for?"

"The Hotel Cortez received an anonymous call. The caller said that he saw someone in a car in the parking lot loading a weapon. The manager called us. The car, a rental, was registered to a man named Childress from Davenport, Iowa."

I waited, trying to look like I wondered what all this had to do with Kearns.

"The manager took us to Childress' room. He was asleep. We changed that. A search of the room discovered several interesting items, including marijuana, peyote buttons, and compelling evidence that he is not named Childress and does not come from Davenport, Iowa."

"Don't tell me," I said.

"Yes," Valencia said, his eyes leaving me for a moment to watch LeDoux schmooze his countrymen. "It was your old punching bag, Elmer Kearns. A further search of his automobile found a weapon, a revolver, rather carelessly hidden under the driver's seat. He appeared to be a great deal more surprised than we were and rather persuasively claims that it isn't his. He said that he's never seen it before and doesn't know how it got there."

I laughed. "Of course, he *would* say that, wouldn't he? I mean, does anybody ever say, 'Oh, hell yes, it's mine? Slap the cuffs on me, officer.'"

Valencia almost smiled. "Not that often. The weapon itself is particularly interesting, among other peculiarities."

"How so?"

"It is an old Smith & Wesson thirty eight, what they used to call a police special, a weapon that once was popular in many of your American television programs."

"Wow, Peter Gunn time," I said, still playing my part to the hilt. Valencia merely looked puzzled. I realized that he didn't know who the hell Peter Gunn was. After explaining that it was a character on an old

TV show, I added, "What I mean is that I haven't seen one of those in years, at least not in real life."

"Assuming that Kearns acquired it here, which he had to since it is virtually impossible to get such a weapon through airport security in Los Angeles, I am puzzled," Valencia said.

"By what?"

"If you know where to go and who to contact, it is not difficult to buy a street weapon here or anywhere. You know that as well as I do. But unless you know what you are doing, and have a trusted contact that knows what he is doing, what you often wind up buying is a cheap, what's the word ... knock ..."

"Knock off?" I suggested. Valencia spoke English so well that I sometimes forgot that it was not his native language.

"Yes, a cheap Chinese knockoff of whatever it is you think you are buying. Someone as ignorant of firearms as Kearns seems to be might think they're getting an AK-47, for example, but what they're really getting is a Chinese replica. It might work well, it might not. But it looks the part."

"But that's not what he had," I said, ever helpful.

"It gets better. The thirty eight was taped so that there are no fingerprints, although the ragged tape was as old as the weapon itself. That is not something usually seen with a street weapon. And the serial number was removed so that it couldn't be traced. It was removed years, probably decades, ago, as best we can tell."

He stopped. I waited.

"You should understand that in my years here, I have never seen a street weapon like this. It is a unique occurrence."

"It is strange, I guess," I agreed. "But strange things happen. We both know that. Logic does not rule."

It was past time to change the subject.

"So what happens to Kearns now?"

"I will send him up to La Paz, since my jail is full of my own people sleeping in shifts so that we can provide security for the movie, and the San Jose del Cabo jail has the people who would normally be in my jail," he said. "Given the false identification, the drugs and the weapon, there is no doubt that he would go to prison if we wished him to."

"If you wished him to? Maybe I'm missing something, but what you've got sounds like a slam dunk."

"The business with the ancient thirty eight is so strange that I might just put him on a flight and send him home, making sure that he can never return to Mexico. It is almost as if someone is trying to frame him."

"Either way he's out of my hair," I said with a big smile. "I'll tell my client. She'll be pleased."

"Yes, I'm sure she will," Valencia agreed, glancing at LeDoux again. "There is one other thing."

"What is that?" I asked.

"Kearns had a second weapon. This one was in his room, cleverly hidden beneath his underwear as if no one would ever think to look there. We actually found it first."

I did not like where this was going.

"A second weapon?"

"Yes a nine millimeter Springfield. You would not believe who it is registered to in the United States."

"Uh, I believe that would be me."

"Such a shocking coincidence," he said "Would you care to tell me about it?"

Since he already knew about my tussle with Kearns, I explained that I had the Springfield on me at the time. When I missed it later, I knew that I must have lost it during the fight, but couldn't very well go back and get it.

"And you didn't see fit to tell anyone?" he asked.

"Who? And what would they have done about it?"

"Telling me would have been a good start," he said. "You would be surprised how much a police department appreciates that kind of information."

I didn't know what to say to that, and had the good sense not to say anything.

"You do see the puzzling aspect to all this," Valencia said.

The man was relentless.

"Not really," I said.

"If Kearns already had a weapon, namely yours, why bother getting another?"

"Maybe he got it before he found mine?"

Valencia shook his head. "There wasn't that much time. He only arrived here late the night before your encounter. Yes, I suppose it is possible, but not likely. You can't just walk into a *mercado* and buy a hand gun."

"I don't really have an answer," I admitted, with good reason. I was so focused on my plan to set up Kearns that I didn't see this complication coming. "Maybe you're being too logical? Kearns doesn't impress me as a great criminal mind, or a great mind period. He's probably a guy who goes where his urges lead him without thinking too much, or at all. Maybe he thought he was Wild Bill Hickok and wanted two guns to wave around and impress girls."

Valencia gave me the hard stare again.

"Why don't you shut up now?"

"Don't I at least get my gun back?"

He didn't even bother to reply.

Fortunately, LeDoux had schmoozed enough. Either that or they ran out of wine. She was ready to go and gave me the high sign. I was more than happy to go with her.

Chapter Nineteen

"How are you doing?"

His voice was calm and carefully modulated, the way it always was. Just listening to him was soothing.

"Things are strange, as usual," I said. "But mostly okay. Well, maybe not. Hell, I don't know."

"I see that there's some confusion. Why don't you tell me about it?'

I'd been seeing, or talking to, the psychiatrist for years. When we lived in Southern California, we'd meet face to face, usually once a week. Since the move to Cabo San Lucas we talked on the phone, although sometimes there were long gaps between conversations. Whenever I got up to Southern California I'd go to his office. When I called and wanted to talk, he always got back to me within a couple of hours. He was a busy and successful professional but still made the time. I appreciated that because I didn't call unless I really needed to. Sometimes I thought about finding a shrink in Cabo so I could do it face to face, but I didn't even know if there was one here and I didn't want to start over anyway.

In the beginning and for a long time, we talked a lot about my parents' brutal murder when I was a boy. I was in their bedroom when two men beat them to death with baseball bats. I know that I saw it happen. The police found me huddled in a corner of the room covered with their blood. But my memory stops just at the critical moment. I obviously repressed the memory and the repression had a lingering effect on me as I grew older. One of the psychiatrist's goals was to get me to recall what happened so I could purge myself of it as much as possible, although I was sure that he'd describe the process in a more sophisticated way. So far, that hadn't happened. I used to have nightmares about it, but it had been a while.

I had other nightmares now.

Since my wife's death in a SCUBA diving accident, one nightmare replaced another. Everything else was pushed so far away that it might as well not exist. Now the only thing that seemed to matter in my life was that Dina wasn't in it. I knew that the psychiatrist was alarmed at some of my behavior since her death, the drifting listlessness that even irritated me, although not enough to do anything about it. But it was never his way to challenge me directly, or to say that something is wrong or right. For one thing, he knew that I'd only resist, which wouldn't do anybody any good, especially me. He often called me a "contrarian." I told him he was wrong.

I explained what I was doing. How I was working for a spoiled actress I didn't like. That was just for starters. I told him about Sterling, LeDoux, Kearns, and the movie. I even told him about the hurricane that I was tired of hearing about.

I told him everything. That was part of the deal.

"Ethan, I'm glad you're working again," he said.

"Why is that?" I knew the answer, but sometimes I wanted to hear how he put it. It had a way of helping me with my own thoughts.

"It's a necessary step for you," he said. "You've taken on clients since Dina's death, but not enough of them to be fully engaged in your changed life."

"I just wish that I liked LeDoux, though. It would make it a lot easier."

"Would it? That may be your way of making excuses so that you can drop the case and retreat back into your shell. Tell me, in the past did liking a client matter very much?"

I'd never thought about it before, at least not in that way.

"Not really, I guess. Most of the time, I didn't know whether I liked or didn't like a client until I was well into the case. When you sign on, all you have are early impressions. And then sometimes my opinion was changed partway through by something they did or I found out. A lot of the time, I barely saw the client. I just did what I did and sent 'em a bill."

There was silence while he thought it over.

"As we have discussed in the past, for you it usually is not about the client, although sometimes it can be a key factor," he said. "It's often more about you taking on the world, a way of defying everyone and everything so you can go your own way and damn the torpedoes."

He chuckled. "You especially seem to enjoy damning the torpedoes, even when they blow up."

"For awful long time, I had someone with me," I said. "I didn't go my own way alone. We faced everything together."

"Yes, but now she's gone. Still, the journey continues, doesn't it? And you are not alone, no matter how you feel. It sounds to me that Valencia did you a big favor, just as you have helped him in the past. Eddie Heenan has helped you, too, several times. I repeat, Ethan, you are not alone. You really can't continue like this."

After her death, I used to have long conversations with Dina about what was going on in my life. Even in death, she helped me work things out. I knew that the conversations were only in my head, but when they stopped I missed them terribly. Hard as it was, the shrink thought it was a good sign that they ended. I wasn't so sure.

We talked about other things, but it was clear that we had covered all the useful ground we would today. Some sessions were good, some were not so good, and most fell somewhere in the middle. I had the feeling that they all helped, even when I couldn't explain how. Sometimes I made fun of it, too. That's what we contrarians do.

"Thanks for not bringing up the hurricane," I said. "Everybody else does."

"I didn't have to," he said. "You did."

Chapter Twenty

She wanted to go out to dinner "like a real person."

I doubted Rio LeDoux knew what that meant anymore. It had been a long time since she behaved or was treated like a real person. Being a real person meant that you didn't just pop into a popular, fully-booked upscale restaurant without a reservation and still be shown to a choice table. Being a real person meant that you actually had to pay for your meal instead of getting it *gratis* just for the pleasure of having your famous face at the restaurant. Being a real person meant that waiters didn't fawn, patrons didn't gape and ordering way off the menu wasn't regarded as a power move and a major pain in the butt.

Under normal circumstances – if there were normal circumstances in her life – taking LeDoux out to dinner like a real person was Sterling's job. Unfortunately, he wasn't around. I could have said no, but since I was being paid to watch her anyway I figured that I might as well go ahead with it.

Cabo San Lucas is one of the most informal places on the planet, so there was no need to dress up. Leaving my shirt tail out conveniently concealed the holstered automatic holstered in front of my hip.

I got to *La Roca* shortly before seven, told the valet that I'd only be a few minutes, and left the Mustang parked in front of the lobby. I hopped an electric cart to LeDoux's pod, told the driver we would be back in just a moment, and rapped on the door.

As usual, LeDoux made everybody wait, but this time it was worth it. Looking good was never a problem for her and that was especially true tonight. With the way it seemed to foam around her knees, her white dress reminded me of the line from Jimmy Webb's song *MacArthur Park*. The golden tan she acquired in Mexico was a beautiful contrast to the dress. The low-cut top wasn't a bad feature either. Her dark hair seemed especially lustrous in the night, like moonlight glistening on water. Whatever cosmetics she wore were so simple, or so expertly applied, it was as if she wasn't wearing any at all and didn't need to.

How someone with this woman's remarkable talent for dissipation managed not to show it was a subject fit for scientists and philosophers to ponder. If I drank as much as she did, I'd either be dead or think I was Millard Fillmore.

The aggressive personality I'd too often seen her wield like a club seemed to be taking a break. Tonight she was soft and almost girlish. Maybe this real person thing really was kind of a treat for her? Or maybe I'm an incurable optimist?

"You look wonderful." She expected me to say it and I was happy to oblige, mostly because she did.

"Thank you." Her smile almost seemed modest. "I do feel good tonight. You know how it is. Some days you don't think much of how you look and some days you do. This is a good day, or a good night, I guess. And it's nice to be with someone who doesn't want something from me, even if it's just for the night."

I twirled an imaginary mustache. "So what makes you think I don't want something?"

She laughed. It was lighthearted, the way laughter should be, not forced, sardonic or sarcastic.

"By now, I'd know if you did. If anything, it's the opposite. I mean, sometimes I think you don't like me at all and hate being around me, even for a little while. And I'll tell you something; a lot of the time I don't blame you."

While that generally described how I felt, it left me wondering why she didn't act like a decent human being more often. But I didn't say anything as I escorted her to the waiting cart, which whisked us to the lobby with its usual electric hum.

It was a pleasantly balmy night, with a light breeze off the water that felt better than medicine. The swirls of stars in the Mexican sky resembled a Van Gogh painting.

We hopped off the cart at the lobby. I tipped the driver and escorted LeDoux to the Mustang. So massive was her self-absorption that although she'd ridden in it just a few days ago - not to mention that I'd followed her from the Rock, to the movie location, and back to the Rock every day that she worked - it was only now that she noticed what I drove.

As I held the passenger door open, she ran her hand along the white leather of the bucket seat.

"This car is so *cool*," she said. "You know, when I was little my Daddy had one of these. He never had the money to restore it like this, but he loved it anyway, a hell of a lot more than he loved us."

Once she settled in, I closed the door and walked around to the driver's side. For such a nice night, I had the top down.

"I can put the top up if you'd like so the wind won't blow your hair."

She shook her head, her dark hair bouncing on her shoulders.

"It's so beautiful tonight. Please leave it down."

Please? Did I just hear Rio LeDoux say please?

As we drove down the dark and winding road to the highway, I said, "I take it that your father doesn't have his Mustang anymore."

"I really don't know, but I doubt it." Her tone indicated that she didn't care either. "He left us when I was little. I didn't see him again until I was rich and famous. And waddaya know, suddenly he was my Daddy and I was his little girl. He was *so* awfully glad to see me. The truth is that he's a worthless jerk who ran away from every responsibility he ever had and some he only made up so he had an excuse to dump us. I told him I never wanted to see or hear from him again."

"But you still call him 'Daddy,'" I said.

She tilted her head back to take in the night and all its starlit glory while she thought about it.

"That's kind of an interesting thing, I guess. I think to most girls your Daddy is always your Daddy, no matter what," she said. "I don't know if it's the same with boys. I might love him, though God knows why, but I sure as hell don't have to like him. I haven't seen him in years. I don't even know if he's still alive."

When we reached the highway, I made a right turn into Cabo. There wasn't much traffic and there was no need to hurry. I had decided to take LeDoux to *Los Barrilas*, on *Calle Miguel Hidalgo* on the far side of town, though "far" doesn't mean much in a little place like Cabo. You can recognize the restaurant by the big barrels over the entrance. There probably was a story there, but I never bothered to find out.

I figured that *Los Barrilas* had several advantages. The food was good, and often better than merely good. It also featured outdoor dining, which was mandatory on a night like this. While it was on a popular pedestrian street with several other restaurants in the block, it had a couple of tables that weren't easily seen from the street, which helped in the realm of privacy. After all, even real people want privacy.

My favorite strolling musician often stopped there, too. Cabo has many such musicians, singles, duos, and groups that wander from restaurant to restaurant, stopping at tables and asking if diners would like a song or two. About half the time for some reason the tourists choose *Guantanamera*, which is actually Cuban, with music put to a poem by Jose Marti. I used to like it, but since moving to Cabo I'd heard it so often that it would be fine with me if I never heard it again. It is understood but never expressed that a donation of a few dollars follows the song. This musician, who was barely five feet tall, wore civilian clothes and did a hysterical version of Elvis Presley's *All Shook Up* in Spanish. He'd even whip out a pair of sunglasses with fake sideburns attached. He had the Elvis leg jiggle going, too. Maybe I'm easily amused, but I enjoyed it every time. The little guy did well with Beatles' songs, too.

Under normal circumstances, it might have been nice to eat at one of the restaurants on Mendano Beach, maybe even at The Office, one of the better known restaurants in Cabo, with our feet in the sand and the water before us. But with one eye on security, I didn't think those restaurants were private enough. Even at night the beach was busy and there were too many power drinkers wandering past on their way to party central somewhere. I didn't want the woman I was supposed to be protecting gawked at by staggering clods with their bellies full of tequila shots.

Villa Serena was another possibility, a beautiful place not far outside of town with a view that gave you the feeling you could see all the way to the mainland. But that restaurant belonged to Dina and me. It was our special place and always would be. I hadn't been back since she died. Maybe one day, but not yet.

Besides, I liked *Los Barrilas* and I was driving.

Chapter Twenty-One

Instead of parking in the centrally located lot at the Wyndham, I opted for street parking, which isn't always easy to find downtown. Again, I wanted to keep the eyeballing of my client to a minimum. After a few minutes nosing around, I found a spot a couple of blocks away on a dark and unpaved street that looked more threatening than it was, which was not at all.

"Jesus, I'm glad I'm not alone," she said, getting out of the car with a nice flash of tanned thigh that seemed to glow in the darkness. "Where the hell are we?"

"Don't worry, little lady, it isn't far," I joked. "I'll protect you."

She put one hand on my shoulder. "You know, I believe you would."

"Unless he's bigger than me, of course," I said. "Then you're on your own."

We laughed as we walked down the street toward the restaurant, her arm linked in mine, just like real people.

At the entrance, she dubiously eyed the barrels.

"Don't ask," I said.

"Why not?"

"Because I don't have an answer."

She playfully punched me in the arm. And so, giggling like a couple of kids, we entered the restaurant.

We were shown to the far corner table that I requested and ordered margaritas while we looked over the menu. I decided on the Drunken Shrimp. She picked Mahi-Mahi with coconut breading and a mango salsa. We both wanted the Caesar Salad, which was prepared at the table. To my mind, it was the best in town. To accompany dinner, we ordered a bottle of Pino Grigio.

We clinked Margarita glasses and sipped while the salad was prepared and served.

"You didn't work today," I said.

"Nobody did." She ran her tongue over her lower lip to capture a drop of margarita, unconsciously making it look like step number eight in a highly successful seduction manual. "Odermeyer's in LA explaining why we're so far behind schedule already. Of course, the director being gone puts us even further behind. They didn't even shoot second-unit stuff today."

"Second unit stuff?"

"Crowd shots, battles scenes, like that."

"So why *are* you so far behind?"

Another sip. "Oh, there are lots of reasons. I've been a pain in the balls, I guess. I don't think that's really slowed us down, but Odermeyer might have a different opinion. It takes forever to get Johnny Miles warmed up, too. That dumbass needs five or six takes just to clear his throat. Odermeyer is known for working pretty slow anyway. And it's a complicated shoot. I always thought the schedule was too ambitious. I think everybody did. My guess is that we'll wind up at least twenty million over budget and it won't be really anybody's fault."

I whistled. "Twenty million? That's real money, even in your business."

The look on her face said that the money issues of large international corporations were not her problem.

"The thing is, it could be really good," she said. "So far, I think I've done my best work ever and Odermeyer really is a good director. I know the story sounds dopy, but we really could have something special, maybe even another *Avatar*."

"Wow!" I said, offering an example of my world famous snappy patter.

"Yeah, major 'wow'," she agreed, setting the empty margarita glass aside and reaching for the wine bottle resting in an ice bucket beside the table. "I need a good 'wow,' too, career-wise, personally-wise, money-wise and pretty much all the wises there are."

75

We finished the salad and sat in silence while our dinner was delivered with a flourish. After the first bite, of Mahi-Mahi, she looked up. "This is *really* good. Thanks for bringing me here."

"My pleasure," I said. "I wasn't sure what to expect, but I'm glad we're here."

She gazed at me over wine glass. "You mean that you didn't know what it would be like to put up with the bitch for the night but couldn't think of a way to get out of it?"

"Well, yeah, something like that," I admitted.

The subject needed changing.

"If you don't mind my asking, how did you get into this business in the first place?"

She put her glass on the table. "You really want to know? It's not a pretty story. I wasn't exactly discovered at Schwab's Drugstore, or something."

"I want to hear it if you want to tell it."

She took a deep breath and dove in.

"After my mother fucked the judge of a little girl talent contest back home in Arkansas, in an amazing coincidence, I won. She did that two more times in bigger competitions until I won a deal to go to LA. I really was a talented little kid and my mother had enough ambition for both of us. When I got a shot I made the most of it. Luck was a big part of it, too. It always is; right place, right time, right projects."

She had warned me; it was not a nice story.

Watching my reaction, she admitted, "Yeah, I know. It's pretty, oh, what's the word ... sordid, isn't it?"

"I don't know about sordid. I think maybe it's just sad. Were you aware of it at the time?" I asked, wondering if I was going too far.

Another sip of Pino Grigio. "Yeah, unfortunately I was. From as far back as I can remember, my mom was more like a sister than a mother. She told me things you should never tell a little kid, especially one of your own children. She did things no parent should ever do, too, and made sure I knew about it, though I don't know why. When I started dating, if that's what you want to call it, sometimes she'd come on to my boyfriends. One time, when I was sixteen, I found out that one guy I really liked was nailing both of us. He was only a year older than me and half her age."

Revolting rather than sordid was the word that came to mind. If LeDoux's mother had suddenly appeared at the table, I might have shot her.

"Where is she now?"

"Dead," LeDoux replied in the same matter-of-fact way she might observe that the mail was late. "She got drunk one night and ran her car off the Pacific Coast Highway."

"I'm sorry."

"Don't be. Between Mommy and Daddy dearest they fucked me up pretty good. I guess I haven't done much to remedy the situation. A shrink told me once that I never had a chance to build up the inner resources to deal with all the bullshit in my life, and I guess he was right. Or maybe I just never wanted to? It's always easier to blame somebody else. That's probably why I'm so good at making excuses. Because of who I am people let me get away with all kinds of stuff. But sometimes I get blamed for things I didn't do or that never happened. I dunno, maybe it all sort of balances out."

"It is kind of weird, though," she added

"What?"

"I know better than anybody what a total shit I can be and then I go ahead and act like it anyway."

Once more, I wanted to ask why she didn't do something about it. But I let it pass again. If she hadn't changed by now it wasn't going to happen. The subject was not in my job description anyway.

"Is the story true about how you got your name?"

She laughed. "You mean about where I was conceived? Not a chance. It's strictly PR, Sterling's idea. I don't think either one of parents could have found Rio on the map."

"Another dream dashed," I said.

"It gets worse." Now that the barriers were down, she was in full confessional mode. "Rio's not my real name; Sterling's idea again. He's been with me almost from the time I got to LA. I liked Rio a lot better than the thing I was born with."

"And that was?"

"Are you ready?"

I took a drink of wine to fortify myself and nodded.

"Okay, let me have it."

"Magenta."

Even if I'd thought of something to say, I was temporarily incapable of speech.

"Magenta LeDoux?" I finally choked out. "That may qualify as child abuse. Where the hell did that come from?"

"I dunno," she admitted. "When I was little, I never had the courage to ask why I had such a damn stupid name. Later, when I changed my name to Rio, it didn't matter. There probably aren't five people in the world who know that."

"So when you got married, however briefly, it was a union of ..."

"That's right," she said. "We were Elmer and Magenta, a marriage made in trailer park heaven."

I decided that called for another glass of wine.

"You said you've been with Sterling a long time?"

"Like I said, from not long after we got to LA. But that's about to change. Don't say anything, but I think I'm gonna have to dump him."

I was surprised to hear that. "Really? Why? He seems to care a lot about you."

She shrugged. "Maybe that's part of the problem. Sometimes it's like he's suffocating me. He's like a mother hen, or something. But at the same time, lately he hasn't earned his keep."

"What do you mean?"

"There were a couple of projects that I *know* I could have hit over the fence. I found out later that they approached Sterling, but he told 'em I wasn't interested without mentioning it to me. When I found out later and reamed him out, he said that they just weren't right for me. Bullshit! I decide what's right for me. At the very least, he should have kept me informed."

"He almost fucked up this one, too," she said. "When he found out they wanted me to read for it, he said no again without telling me. He claimed that somebody of 'my stature' shouldn't have to audition. He knows damn well that my stature ain't what it used to be. I begged a lot, they let me read, and I got it, no thanks to Sterling. Sometimes it's like he doesn't want me to grow."

"Does he know what you're going to do?"

"Not yet, though I'm pretty sure he suspects that something's up. I'm gonna wait until after the shoot before I tell him. It'll be a big drama and I don't need the distraction right now."

She ran her finger around the top of her wine glass. "It's funny, but Elm's been telling me to get rid of Sterling for years."

"Elm?"

"Elmer, my ex." She rolled her eyes. "You know, the one you *saved* me from."

"Oh," I said, "good old Troy."

She giggled. "Okay, the name thing was a dumb idea. Nobody said he was the brightest guy in the word. He tried getting into the business just to stay around me, name change and all, but gave up a long time ago. After all these years, he's still seriously in love with me. The thing is, everybody's got the wrong idea about him. They think he's bad for me, but he's really not after anything. Not money, not anything. The truth is that I'm probably bad for him. The drugs are all my fault. They say I have an addictive personality and I sort of drag him along. I'm glad you didn't hurt him. I know I shouldn't go back to him the way I do sometimes, but it's nice to know he's always there. He's so devoted that he's like a dog, or something. He doesn't give a shit that I'm a movie star. Mostly he wants to protect me. He thinks the business is bad for me, that Sterling is a controlling asshole, and he wants me to give it up and go away with him. But can you see me as Mrs. Nobody in Fresno, or someplace? I don't fuckin' think so."

"No, I guess not," I said. 'Sterling said that Kearns broke into your house a while back. You don't find that alarming?"

"I don't know what the hell he's talking about. That doesn't sound like Elm at all."

"Maybe," I said. "People who think they're in love do strange things sometimes."

I sympathized with LeDoux more than I had before tonight, but that didn't mean I liked her. There was nothing in the conversation that was about anything other than herself. When we talked about other people, or anything at all, it was about how everything and everyone related to her. All Rio, all the time.

It was as if she lived in a world surrounded by mirrors. No matter where she looked, all she saw was herself and that was all that mattered.

Chapter Twenty-Two

The evening passed quickly, so quickly that a man grew out of the tree on the other side of the wall that surrounded the restaurant courtyard.

The cinder block wall was about eight feel tall and the tree with its wide-spreading limbs grew ten or twelve feet higher. The photographer must have entered the restaurant next door, passed the management a little cash to look the other way, and climbed the tree where he was industriously snapping away at the two of us.

Sitting with her back to him, LeDoux didn't know he was there and I debated whether to tell her. After all, the photos couldn't be that exciting. But I knew that where there was one there would be more, if not now, then soon. She should be told to avoid unpleasant surprises.

"Rio, don't turn around," I said. "But there's a guy with a camera in the tree in back of you on the other side of the wall."

The woman who was so buoyant all evening deflated before my eyes.

"Shit! It's been such a nice night, too."

"I assume there will be more of them eventually," I said.

"Oh, yeah," she agreed. "They're like locusts. Dammit! How many pictures of me do they need?"

"Just the one that catches you doing something you shouldn't be doing: Maybe he hopes we'll get into an argument and you'll slap me, or something. Do you want to go?"

"Yeah, we probably should."

I did feel sorry for her. I couldn't imagine what it must be liked to be constantly dogged like this. A few minutes earlier, she had told me about the time she attended a charity fundraiser at the Beverly Hilton and went to the bathroom. When she entered a stall, a woman in the next stall shoved her cell phone under the partition to get some snappy photos of Rio LeDoux on the can.

"What did you do?"

"I pulled up my knickers, marched into her stall, kicked her ass and trashed her phone. The bitch sued me. I paid a hundred grand to keep it out of court, but it was worth it."

I asked for the check and paid it. But our getaway was already too late. A clutch of aggressive paparazzi had already gathered on the street in front of the restaurant. Although the Mustang was only a couple of blocks away, getting there with LeDoux would be like running a gauntlet. Hanging around her, I'd already seen how they tried to provoke her into losing her temper. It usually didn't take much.

A check with the waiter revealed that there was no back exit.

"I'll get the car and bring it out front," I said. "When you hear me honk you run outside and get in. Don't stop moving, don't say anything, and don't do anything. Just put your head down and keep going. I'll have the door open. You slide in and we're off."

As plans go, it wasn't great but we were trapped and it was the best we could do. By now there were at least a dozen paparazzi on the street. They were even making it hard for traffic to pass.

This was no time to be polite. I didn't feel like it anyway. I shot out of *Los Barrilas* like an NFL running back. I hit the mob of photographers with my shoulder lowered and knocked two of them out of my way in a hail of curses and fulminations. I easily left them behind as I rounded the corner and ran to the Mustang. After all, it wasn't me they were interested in.

There was nobody on the dark street when I opened the door, slid behind the wheel, started the car and hit the gas. In a few seconds I screeched to a halt in front of the restaurant, where there was an even bigger crowd than when I left a couple of minutes ago, including a lot of tourists who stopped to rubberneck. They didn't know what was going on but they wanted to see it anyway. Their presence only added to the chaos. I felt a dark mood building.

My plan was shot to hell. Despite the restaurant staff's efforts to keep them out, four paparazzi had LeDoux boxed in at the table. She was getting bombed with blinding flashes while trying to shield her eyes with her hands. There was no reason for them to do it except torture. I shoved my way to her side and put my arm around her shoulders. She couldn't see who it was and fought against me until I whispered in her ear. "It's me, Ethan. Time to get out of here."

It was hard to make progress against the human tide. I could have barreled through the lot of them again, but having LeDoux with me made that impossible. Some of the paparazzi were so close they must have been trying to get a shot of her nose hairs.

Before we got to the car, one guy who carried a Nikon with a barrel lens got so close that it banged LeDoux's forehead. She cried out and sagged. I caught her before she fell.

Something in me erupted. The paparazzi with the camera that hit her had it hanging around his neck from a leather strap. He was using another one without a long lens to shoot. I grabbed the Nikon, pulled it the length of the strap, and then smashed him in the face with it. He yelled and staggered back with what I hoped was a broken nose. That gave me a little space. It was like shooting fish in a barrel. Most of the paparazzi were something less than prime physical specimens and my anger was all I needed as I lashed out. I seized one that I'd put down by his wrist and ankle and swung him around in giant circles, clearing an opening that allowed LeDoux to get into the Mustang.

Around and around we went until I let go and sent him sailing into the mob, taking several of his peers down with him, kind of like human bowling.

I slid into the driver's seat and hit the gas with a screech of tires. At the next block, I turned right, and then right again. After one more right, I took a back road out of town, with nobody following that I could see.

I wanted until we were on the highway on the way to *La Roca* before I reached over to LeDoux.

"Are you okay?"

"Fuck! Fuck! Fuck! Fuck! Fuck! FUCK!"

I couldn't agree more.

Chapter Twenty-Three

When we got back to LeDoux's pod at *La Roca*, I examined her forehead where the camera hit her.

She had a ding that might bruise, but she wasn't bleeding. It was nothing that a little artfully applied makeup couldn't fix. In a day or two, no one would even know it was there.

Shaken and crying, she curled up on the leather couch, which was when she started to laugh, the last thing I expected.

"Glad to see you're feeling better." I went to the bar and poured two shots of tequila, one for her and one for me. "But what's so funny?"

By now, the flow of tears came entirely from laughter. I knew that it was just the release of nervous tension, the residue of a wild adrenalin rush back at the restaurant, but it still seemed pretty strange under the circumstances.

"OK, Rio, it's time to share with the rest of the class," I said, taking a sip of the tequila. "What's so damn funny?"

With all of her laughter, by now she was gasping for air. "That guy ... that guy ... you threw him like a Frisbee, or something ... I've never seen anything ... it was the funniest ...."

With a feeble wave, she gave up and laughed some more.

After a few minutes, she settled down and handed me her empty glass for another tequila shot. I obliged her but didn't pour one for myself. There had already been enough alcohol this night.

"Here you go," I said, returning the full glass. "Now that you're okay, I'd better get going."

She was off the couch and on me like a limpet mine, except this limpet mine had a great body and least six hands, all of them clawing at my clothes while removing her own. Multi-tasking at its best.

"Make love to me. I'll do anything you want. Please. Please. Make love to me. Love me. Just love me"

These tender endearments were whispered into my ear with the force of a category five hurricane. I was supposed to find it seductive, but this sad wreck of a woman only repelled me. The sorrow I felt earlier disappeared in an instant. Maybe some of the mess she'd become wasn't her fault, but a lot of it was. If she was a victim, she was a willing victim who used her miserable upbringing as an excuse for her awful behavior.

At this moment, Rio LeDoux, one of the most desirable women in the world, was about as alluring as a succubus. I was afraid that if I stayed she'd drain all the life out of me.

By now she had her dress pooled around her feet and was down to her panties. With my professional eye for detail, earlier in the evening I'd noticed that she wasn't wearing a bra. With all the ripping and tearing, she'd done away with my shirt buttons, too. I grabbed her wrists and held them so she couldn't do any more wardrobe damage. It wasn't easy. She was a big woman and stronger than she looked.

"Rio, I can't ... *we* can't. You're just feeling vulnerable right now. This is a really bad idea for both of us. Having sex with a client is impossible."

Actually it was very possible. But not now, and not with *this* client. Not ever.

"I know you want to," she moaned, trying escape my grasp so she could claw at me again. "I can tell. Just let me make love to you. I'll do everything. Please! No one will ever know but us, I promise."

"NO!" I gave her a shove, a gentle shove, but a shove nonetheless.

Caught off balance, she staggered back and glared at me with equal parts surprise and anger. She was breathing hard. So was I.

Suddenly everything about her changed. It was almost demonic.
"Get out! Get out! GET OUT!"

Her face was wet and contorted and her eyes were wild as she snarled, kicking and punching. If any of the kicks and punches connected, I didn't feel it.

I got out.

Chapter Twenty-Four

The next morning, I was famous, or maybe infamous.

I should have seen the media storm coming. But it didn't even occur to me until I listened to a message from Eddie Heenan. He said that in his opinion the paparazzi toss had real possibilities for the next Olympic Games. My form needed work, but I showed potential.

I didn't bother to call back.

Chango Suarez, a retired southern California police detective and the toughest man I've ever known, called to observe that I really must be as stupid as he always thought I was. What the hell was I thinking anyway, assuming that I was thinking at all? How did it feel to set private detecting back a thousand years?

Valencia called to compliment me on the subtlety of my approach and how I was an inspiration to everyone in law enforcement all over the world. After what happened last night, the paparazzi and their legions of lawyers wanted me drawn and quartered. But he said that they rarely did that kind of thing in Mexico anymore and I shouldn't worry about it too much.

Tony Suarez, one of Chango's many sons, an ex-cop turned lawyer in San Francisco Bay area, and someone I'd worked with before, called to say that if I needed a good lawyer I should *not* call him under any circumstances. And by the way, he was changing his telephone number.

Several alleged news organizations wanted to interview me. One particularly odious operation offered $50,000 for story exclusivity and much more than that if I was willing to collaborate on a book with one of their writers.

Out of curiosity, I Googled myself. How bad could it be, I thought?

It was pretty bad.

What happened at the restaurant probably only seemed like it was everywhere, including in many languages that I couldn't read. There probably were distant parts of the globe that didn't give a damn. I just couldn't find them. My favorite photograph was of me in mid-paparazzi toss. He was sailing through the air toward his compatriots with a terrified look on his face, I had a nice follow through, and a cowering Rio LeDoux was getting into the Mustang like she was fleeing from a bank robbery gone wrong. I was variously identified as "Rio's secret lover," the "Hollywood bad girl's Cabo boy friend," and "a controversial private eye with a dark and sordid past." We were, one website declared, "Caught in a love tryst."

I didn't mind "a dark and sordid past," but "love tryst?" Really? Do people still have those things? The spirit of Hedda Hopper is alive and well.

My background was hashed out, and mostly hashed up, sometimes so badly that I didn't recognize myself. One story identified me as Nathan Crankshot. A spokesman for the movie studio in Los Angeles said that the "unfortunate incident" in Cabo San Lucas would be carefully examined and appropriate action taken, whatever that meant. The whole thing was widely characterized as yet another problem for "an already troubled production and a long troubled star."

Rio LeDoux and her representative had no comment. Ominously.

In short, everything that could go wrong did go wrong. I had committed, with great enthusiasm, exactly the kind of thing I was hired to help avoid and managed to get world-wide publicity while doing it.

I probably wouldn't put this one on my resume.

Chapter Twenty-Five

"You're fired! Do you understand me, Cruickshank? You're through!"

Sterling was out of sorts. Under the circumstances, I couldn't blame him.

When he learned about what happened at the restaurant last night, he said that he flew down to Cabo on a rented private jet, the better to begin damage control.

Not to mention ream me out in person.

We were in LeDoux's place at *La Roca*, although there was no sign of her.

"Rio's working and she wants nothing more to do with you after last night," Sterling announced. "Neither do I."

He was walking around the living room in frantic little circles, probably not even aware of what he was doing, and waving his arms like he was flagging a jet into the terminal.

"What the hell is wrong with you? A fight? In public? At a restaurant? With paparazzi? Why don't you just set Rio up so she's caught smuggling drugs? This is the most incompetent thing I've ever seen. It's exactly what we wanted to avoid."

"Listen, Sterling, it wasn't what it looks like. I ..."

"I don't care!" he shouted. "You still don't get it, do you? In this business, what it looks like is all that matters. It's everything! Even when Rio blames it all on you – and I intend to make sure that she does when I put together a statement – no one is going to believe her."

Sterling stopped in mid-stride as a thought struck him.

"Wait a minute! Cruikshank, it just occurred to me. What were you doing out with her anyway?"

He thought about it and then gave me his best tough guy look. He made a fist and everything. I remained calm.

"Don't tell me you took advantage of that poor kid? Is that really what this is all about? As vulnerable as she is right now, are you really *that* low, Cruickshank?"

Considering what happened last night in this room, the conversation, one-sided as it was, had taken a turn for the macabre. And kid? Really? Is that how he saw her?

"Did I take advan ..." The thought was such lunacy that I could barely speak. "Sterling, you've *got* to be kidding. The French Foreign Legion couldn't take advantage of that woman."

"Don't you dare blame Rio for your incompetence, or, by God, I'll kick your ass myself!"

I laughed out loud. I shouldn't have, but couldn't help it. I was either a stunning incompetent or I was clever enough to take advantage of poor, helpless Rio LeDoux, but I couldn't be both. Besides, he just fired me. What could he do now?

My laughter infuriated Sterling even more, but it didn't matter. He was many things, but an ass kicker he was not. For one thing, it might ruffle his hair. He could always hire somebody to do it, but I doubted even that.

Apparently he thought better of the ass kicking strategy.

"I'll send you a check for your work to this point, not that you earned it," he said, still seething. "Now get out!"

This was the second time in less than twenty-four hours I was thrown out of the same room.

When I've got a good thing going, I stay with it.

I got out.

Chapter Twenty-Six

As I waited in front of the *La Roca* lobby for the Mustang to be brought around from the parking garage, Danny Lieber sauntered up, wearing his smirk like a new suit.

"Thought I'd come hang out with a celebrity," he said. "Kind of bask in your glow."

"I don't do autographs," I said.

"You've had a tough couple of days."

"The hell of it is they're right. I should have handled it better," I admitted. "I blew up and did everything wrong."

"From what I heard, under the circumstances I'm not sure there was a right way, but I'm sorry you got fired, EC," he said. "You didn't deserve the chewing out either."

The valet brought up the Mustang, but Lieber's comment stopped me before I got in.

"Wait a minute! How did you know I got chewed out and fired? It just happened a few minutes ago."

Lieber's face told me that he knew he'd said too much.

I stared at him, putting it all together.

"You've got LeDoux's place wired, don't you?"

After looking around to make sure that no one could hear, Lieber stepped up close, just to make sure.

"Yeah, we do, though nobody calls it wired anymore," he admitted, keeping his voice down so no one else could hear. "You're about a generation behind on that one. It's one part of the security system in that pod that I, uh, didn't mention. It's not just for LeDoux; it's for everybody who stays there. In case something happens and there are liability issues, we'll know what really went on."

For some reason, I wasn't surprised. In the world we live in, privacy is an increasingly rare commodity.

"But that can't be admissible, not even in a Mexican court," I said.

"It doesn't have to be admissible," Lieber explained. "If something happens and somebody's lying about it, we'll know it. If it becomes necessary, we'll let them know we know it, along with what we might do with the information. It doesn't have to be official or legal to be effective. You know that. It's just another level of protection for us. You'd be surprised at some of the stuff that goes on here."

""Probably not," I said. "You have visual, too?"

Lieber shook his head. "We thought about it, but that's too invasive. We're not out to hurt anybody or threaten our guests. We don't want to get sued either. We're just trying to protect ourselves. Besides, these days that kind of stuff has a way of going public, with sex tapes and everything. That's a headache we don't need."

"So you must have heard what happened last night between me and LeDoux," I asked.

He looked sheepish, something I'd never seen in the man.

" 'Fraid so. Sorry, EC. You just got caught in the middle."

I got in the Mustang and cranked it up. Before I could put it in gear, Lieber put his hands on the door and leaned into the car, speaking just loud enough to be heard over the thrum of the engine.

"EC, if you ask me you should have banged her when she begged you to," he said. "I mean, the way things turned out, it wouldn't have made any difference, would it?"

Without bothering to answer, I put the Mustang in gear and drove away.

With friends like that ....

Chapter Twenty-Seven

It turned out that my newfound notoriety was good for business. It reminded a lot of people that I was still around and piqued the interest of many other people I didn't know, and probably didn't want to. It didn't hurt that the paparazzi shots all over the Internet made me look like the toughest guy since John L. Sullivan.

The first day, I got seven contacts from people who were convinced they needed a private detective and wanted me in particular. Via email, text, and phone, I also got two proposals of marriage from women I'd never met, three offers of fulltime employment, several opportunities from dubious news organizations around the world to tell "my side" of the story, whatever that meant, and a contact from a guy who swears that he sat behind me in third grade and wanted to "catch up on old times."

One of the jobs was easy, so naturally I took it. A skip tracer I know in Phoenix was looking for a bail jumper and thought he might have run to southern Baja, maybe Cabo San Lucas. He wasn't sure enough to justify the trip down himself, so he emailed some photos and a sheet and asked if I'd check it out. It only took a half day to run the guy down. It turned out that he'd come here a couple of weeks ago and was selling time shares under his real name.

It's not generally known, but finding people is often just that easy. Most people don't have a clue how to obtain false identification, at least not quickly, and especially not in a strange place. But, unless they're wealthy, they've still got to eat and have to use their real names to get work. They also tend to run to places they know, and this guy had been to Cabo four times in six years.

I called my contact in Phoenix and explained where the runner could be found, without mentioning how easy it was to find him. My reputation as a miracle worker could always use some boosting. If I kept my mouth shut, which I fully intended to do, the skip tracer could tell his client that he did it all himself via the usual brilliant investigative techniques. We agreed to split the fee. Easy money.

Two other jobs seemed like they might be interesting, but there was no urgency to either one. I told the callers that I'd look into what they wanted. If I thought I could help, I'd let them know within twenty-four hours. If I couldn't help, I'd recommend someone who could. They seemed satisfied with that.

As things turned out, I never got the chance.

Chapter Twenty-Eight

I was on my way to the tennis club when I got a call. When I saw who it was, I put the phone on speaker, pleased once again that I had the Mustang retrofitted with all the modern trappings, at least those I understood.

"Cruickshank, it's Odermeyer, the director." Opposed, I guess, to Odermeyer the butcher, the baker, or the candlestick maker. "Is anybody with you?"

"Nope. I'm in my car all by myself. There's no one but the two of us and you're not really here. So how's the glamorous world of movies?"

"Not so good lately," he said. "One of our stars has disappeared."

"I assume you're talking about LeDoux."

"Of course, who else?"

"Why am I not surprised? Exactly what do you mean, disappeared?"

"Disappeared as in vanished. We can't find her. She isn't anywhere, at least not anywhere we've looked and, believe me, we've looked everywhere we can think of. Nothing. Nada. Zilch."

I wanted to concentrate on the conversation so I pulled off to the side of the road, narrowly avoiding a cactus.

"You do know that she's done this before, right?" I said. "I mean, she has a whole history of it. She even did it to me, though she didn't get far."

"Yeah, I know, that's one reason I called you." Odermeyer didn't sound good; a man on the verge of collapse, with a tremor in his voice that I could hear over the cell phone. "This one feels different than the others. I don't know how to explain, but I don't think it's the usual bullshit. And here's the kicker: We can't find Sterling either."

"I just saw him the other day," I said. "Are you telling me that nobody at his office knows where he is?"

"There's nobody *in* his office. When I called several times and got no answer, I had a friend go over to Sterling's office in Century City. He wasn't there. Nobody was. He's not at home either. His housekeeper answered the door, but said she hasn't seen or heard from him in a while. She wasn't worried about it because he travels a lot anyway. He's still registered at the resort here, but nobody's seen him. It's the same with Rio."

"Odermeyer, you do know they fired me, right?"

"Yeah, I know," he said. "And I know why, too. It wasn't your fault. But *I'm* hiring you, if you'll take it on. Whatever they paid you, I'll pay you."

"Paying expensive private detectives to look for missing stars and their stooges can't be in your budget."

"Let me worry about that. The words miscellaneous expense covers a lot of ground, especially in this business."

"Where are you?"

"On location, but we can't meet here. Too many people. Everybody knows you got fired and if they saw you around here again they'd start asking questions. Let's have a drink somewhere. I could use one. Or five."

I gave him directions to La Gaviota, my tennis and fitness club. It had a nice bar and small restaurant overlooking the gulf, a place conducive to private conversation. As far as I knew, none of the movie people had discovered it.

"Is a half hour okay," he asked. "We need to get moving."

"It's fine with me. I was headed there anyway."

I waited for a tractor-trailer rig to rumble past, then pulled back onto the road and hit the gas. My head snapped back as the Mustang roared away. I wanted get there early. There was a lot to think about.

Chapter Twenty-Nine

As shaky as he sounded over the phone, Odermeyer looked even worse.

He was skinny on the fattest day he ever had and still looked like he'd lost weight, although such a thing didn't seem possible. He didn't have bags under his eyes; he had an entire set of luggage. He was slow and stooped as he approached the table at La Gaviota where I waited. The weight of massive responsibility gone wrong was breaking him down. I didn't know how old he was, but I bet he looked at least ten years older.

Maybe every movie was like this? For his sake, I sure as hell hoped not.

I already had a *Negra Modelo* on the table on front of me. Odermeyer ordered a rum and coke with lime. When it arrived, he drained it in about five seconds and immediately ordered another. Not for the first time, I concluded that movie people drank a lot.

"So tell me about it," I said.

"When Rio didn't show up on time, I thought she was just late again. I mean, hell, she's almost always late. But this time she *never* showed up. That's never happened before. I called her cell, but it went straight to message. I tried email and texting her, too. I even tried twitter to see if she was active. She wasn't."

He took a big gulp of his second drink. I figured that I had to get the story out of him quickly, while he was still coherent.

"When she no-showed the second day, I called again with the same result. I tried to contact Sterling, but he didn't answer or get back to me either. Like I told you before, he was still registered at his resort, just like Rio at *La Roca*. I left messages at the desk, both places. It was the same thing at his Century City office; no answer and no return call. I had a friend in LA go to his office and then to his house in Bel Air. Nothing doing, just like at Rio's house in the Hollywood Hills. I don't like it, but I do kind of get it with Rio. It wouldn't be the first time she's done something like this. But Sterling has a business to run. Where the hell is his secretary? What about his staff and his other clients?"

"What does the studio say?"

"Nobody there knows yet."

"How are you pulling that off?"

"We're shooting around Rio. But I can't keep it up forever. Sooner or later, somebody's gonna rat us out, or we'll run out of make work. Then it'll become a big deal, a very big deal. They'll shut the movie down and if that happens Rio's career goes down the toilet. Maybe she deserves it, but I don't think she's really that bad; no worse than some I've worked with. But the other thing is that a lot of hard working people associated with the movie who didn't do anything wrong won't get paid. People think that the movies make you rich. A few *do* get rich, but not the rank and file. They'll just get screwed."

I hadn't heard the phrase "rat us out" since Jimmy Cagney said it in black and white.

"What about you?"

Odermeyer took another swallow of his rum and coke and gazed off into the distance. The water looked good today, nice and peaceful, unlike his world of late. As Anthony predicted, the hurricane had veered off. But there was another one out there already and it was barreling our way, though you couldn't tell it by the scene before us.

The silence was punctuated by the thwock of somebody hitting tennis balls nearby. I always liked that sound, especially when I created it, and the pleasant jolt that ran up your arm when you did it right. There was nothing quite like it.

"Thanks for asking, but I'll be fine," he replied. "Short term, it won't do me a helluva lot of good. It's never good to be associated with disaster. But I have a solid track record, I'm well known in the business, and I'll be okay. Right or wrong, most of the blame's gonna fall on Rio, assuming something bad didn't happen to her. It may not be fair, but that's how it'll go. With her reputation, she'll wind up guilty whether or not she really is."

Odermeyer drained the last of his drink. "Like I said, this time it feels different, especially with Sterling disappearing, too. It's too weird. There's something going on."

When the waiter asked he wanted another rum and coke, Odermeyer waved him away. He had enough and he knew it. I had underestimated him. I was glad because I liked him. I'd only finished half my beer and didn't want another one. I didn't even want the half I drank.

"So will you help me?"

Before I could answer, he held up a warning hand.

"Before you say anything, remember, you can't tell anyone what you're doing or why you're doing it, at least not until word gets out, *if* it gets out. I know that'll make your job harder, but it can't be helped. I've got to keep this quiet for as long as I can."

So there it was, lying there waiting to be picked up by Ethan Cruickshank, Private Idiot. I couldn't believe that I was about to do what I was about to do.

"Sure, I'll give it a shot," I said. "File it under miscellaneous expense. Lot of that going around."

Chapter Thirty

I needed to take a look at LeDoux's pod at the Rock and to check out Sterling's room at El Grande Cabo. I also needed more information on Sterling. Odermeyer was right. The double disappearance was no coincidence.

When someone goes missing, the rule is to check out family and close friends first. I considered putting Anthony on it but decided to do it myself. He was good for pure information but the human factor was missing.

I already knew that Rio LeDoux had no siblings and her mother was dead. That left dear old Dad and Elmer Kearns. LeDoux claimed that Kearns was harmless, but didn't mean he was. He didn't seem harmless when he tried to kick me in the head.

It didn't take me long to learn that Cletus LeDoux had taken up residence in a federal penitentiary three years ago. If he was a good boy, he might get out in two more. From what I saw and heard, it was some kind of financial scam in which LeDoux wasn't the man, just the man left holding the bag. He was a small timer who tried to swim with the sharks and got eaten.

Next I called Eddie Heenan, who had the human factor up the wazoo.

"Eddie, I need some information on Alton Sterling and Elmer Kearns."

"That should be easy enough," he said. "What's going on?"

I ignored the question. "What I need is anything and everything. What does Sterling do exactly and how does he do it? Who are his clients? Does he have a family? Is anybody unhappy with him? Does he fondle sheep? What about his finances? As for Kearns, I need to know where he is now and what he's been up to lately. Anything you find, I want."

"Ethan, if I knew what you're doing and why you're doing it, it'd help me set priorities and save a lot of blundering around," he said.

He was right, of course. Knowing why you're looking helps clarify what you're looking for.

"That's the problem, Eddie," I admitted. "I can't tell you. I'd like to, but I can't."

Sometimes nothing is as loud as silence. This was one of those times.

Finally he said, "Okay, I'll do it. I assume you need it ASAP since you always do. You'll tell me later what this is all about, right?"

"If I can. I owe you, Eddie."

"What else is new?"

Next I called Danny Lieber.

"Danny, it's payback time," I said.

"Jeez, that was fast," he grumbled. "After the other day when you figured it out about LeDoux's place, I knew it'd come around sometime, but I assumed sometime was a ways down the road. So what is it? What do I have to do to get outta the hole?"

"I need to get into LeDoux's place."

Before he could protest, I explained by lying.

"She's out of town for a while and won't even know I was there. There's no harm in it for her, for you, or for *La Roca*. But one way or another, I've got to get in."

"Why? What the hell's going on?"

"I can't tell you. You're just going to have to trust me. You can be there with me if it makes you feel better."

"EC, I'm not sure I wanna stand there and watch you go through her underwear, or whatever it is you're gonna be doing in there," he said. "It'd be better if I didn't know anyway. Make it easier to deny if something goes south."

He thought about it a little longer.

"Okay, how about if I wait outside, someplace where it doesn't draw attention? That way I can make sure you're not interrupted. I can probably give you a half hour. Maybe I can even stretch that a little. But that's all you get. Agreed? Anything longer is just too risky. If *La Roca* ever found out, I'd lose my job. And remember, if you get caught, you're on your own. Got it?"

"I understand," I promised. "All I have to do is not get caught. Hell, who's going to catch me? You're the head of security. By the way, can you shut down the audio so no one can hear me when I'm inside?"

"Yeah, I can do that, I guess. Me and my big mouth."

Once we set a time the next day for my visit to *La Roca*, I called a housekeeper I knew who was on the staff at Sterling's resort, *El Grande Cabo*. Before she got a job there, Rosa was our housekeeper for a couple of years. A while back, her son fell in with some bad people. I got him out of trouble and she's been grateful to me ever since. After Dina's death, she called several times to see how I was doing and always asked if she could help in any way.

I hated to do what I was about to do, but with two people missing I didn't have time for finesse.

"Rosa, it's Ethan Cruickshank."

"Mister Ethan! How are you?"

The fact that she was so glad to hear from me made me feel even guiltier than I already did.

"Rosa, I need a favor, a big favor. If you can't do it, or think you might get in trouble, just tell me no and I'll understand."

I can be duplicitous as hell when it's necessary. I knew my saying that would make her even more inclined to help me, no matter the possible consequences.

"Mister Ethan, I am so happy that at last I can do something for you. I will do anything you ask."

When I told her what I wanted, she didn't hesitate or ask why. I arranged to meet her at her little house when she got off work and pick up a card key that would get me into Sterling's suite at *El Grande Cabo*.

Which I did.

And felt terrible about it.

Chapter Thirty-One

I wanted to hear from Heenan before taking a look at where Sterling and LeDoux were staying in Cabo. Whatever information he found might give me some context. Fortunately, he called early the next morning.

"You're pretty fast when you want to be," I said.

"Curiosity is a hell of a motivator. I figure the sooner I get back to you the sooner you'll tell me what this is all about."

"I admire optimism," I said. "So what have you got?"

"Ethan, you're not gonna believe this."

"Try me."

"Sterling doesn't have any other clients. Rio Ledoux is it. He barely has a business."

"What do you mean he barely has a business?"

"Over the last two years, Alton Sterling gradually separated himself from every one of his clients except her."

"Separated himself? They didn't dump him?"

"You could say that he dumped them," Heenan explained. "From what I hear, he told them his business had grown so much that it was bigger than he wanted it to be, that he preferred more of a nimble boutique-style operation. He didn't want to hire more people, but, at the same time, he was so busy that he didn't feel that he could do right by some of the clients he had."

"Anyway, Sterling strongly suggested that they find other representation, which, over time, they did. Not some of them. All of them, except LeDoux. The guy doesn't even have a fulltime secretary or a staff anymore. He let them all go. He has a temp to make it look like he's still cookin' along. But she's only part-time."

"But why would he do that?" I asked. "And why didn't anybody notice?"

"Like I told you before, everybody knew that he was winding down, but not like this. He did a good job hiding the extent of it, too, with a lot of phony PR about projects that never existed. Mostly nobody noticed because nobody cared about Sterling's client list."

"What about his family? They can't be happy about it."

"Sterling doesn't have a family. He was married for a while, but divorced eight years ago, with no kids. She remarried, moved to Bumfuck, Washington, someplace, and doesn't have any contact with him. He paid alimony for a while but that stopped when she remarried."

"Eddie, this is damned strange stuff," I said. "What's your take on all this?"

"From the looks of things, I think he devotes himself to Rio LeDoux twenty-four/seven. What I don't know is why he gave the rest of it up."

"When he was down here in Cabo, he kept going back to LA on business," I said

"I dunno about that, but I'm guessing it was mostly show, if he really went back at all. I mean, maybe he did have some Rio stuff to do, but it's probably nothing he couldn't do down there. And I guarantee that he doesn't *have* other business, even if he wants people to think he does. On the surface, he's as busy and successful as ever. I checked his financials, at least what I could get to fast, and that's in the shit can, too, mostly thanks to Rio. Over the last couple of years, he's given her more than four million dollars."

"You said 'given.' Not loaned or advanced?"

"It's on Sterling's books as payment, but it isn't. My guess is that he tells her it's residuals, or delayed payment for earlier projects, or something like that. Trust me, it's not. She hasn't done that well lately. The money didn't come from anywhere but his own pocket. He's carryin' her and he's been doin' it for a while with diminishing resources."

"Eddie, how'd you find all this out? It's reliable, right?"

"Lotta people owe me favors. And, like I said, Sterling's office is empty most of the time. I'm surprised he hasn't given it up or moved to a smaller place. Probably the prestige location is part of the smoke. Where he is in Century City demands primo rent. There's nobody but a temp who works maybe twenty hours a week. Mostly she answers the phone, handles walk-ins, and works on her nails."

"So you telling me you broke into his office?"

"Of course, I broke into his office. You said you needed whatever I could get as soon as I got it and that was the fastest way. Sterling's pretty careless with private information. He had some in a wall safe, but that was easy to crack. The rest of it had no security at all; mostly in his computer and stuff in file drawers, the old fashioned way. I don't think he gives a damn anymore. I don't know why or what changed him, but it sure as hell looks that way."

There was a lot of information to digest. It might have been easier if it made sense.

"There's one more thing," he said.

"What?"

"Alton Sterling isn't his real name."

Now that Heenan brought it up, that *did* made sense. In or around the movie business, people change their names all the time. I mean, who the hell is really named Alton Sterling?

"What is it?" I asked.

"Harold Lipschitz. He's from someplace in Jersey."

"Harold Lipschtiz?" I said. "Oh, why the hell not? Half the people I've run into on this case don't use their real names. I might change mine to Sam Spade."

"You'd look ugly as hell in a fedora," Heenan said. "So do you want me to keep lookin'?"

"Yeah, I do. Try to find out if anyone's seen Sterling lately, or had contact with him; phone, email, text, Facebook, twitter, tooter, anything. Check his phone records, too, if you can. And his credit cards. You got enough friends who owe you favors to do all that?"

Heenan didn't bother to answer. He had a question of his own.

"Ethan, are you sayin' that Sterling's gone? As in disappeared or on the run?"

"I didn't say that."

"What about Rio?"

"I didn't say anything about her either."

"Yeah, you're a man of few words. By the way, am I gettin' paid for this?"

"Miscellaneous expense," I said.

Heenan snorted. "OK, I'll check out Kearns next."

Chapter Thirty-Two

I met Lieber at *La Roca* an hour later. We boarded a cart and headed for LeDoux's pod.

When we arrived, he slipped me a card key and a duplicate of the cuff bracelet with the turquoise buttons he gave to LeDoux.

"I'm gonna park up here a ways and stroll around like I'm patrolling the grounds," he explained. "I do that sometimes to keep everybody on their toes. When the staff sees me they won't think anything of it."

He gave me a long look. "Make it fast, EC."

"Words to live by," I said over my shoulder, already heading toward the door.

Once I was inside, I stood still in the living room and let my senses take over.

The stillness was palpable, the way it always is in an empty place when you shouldn't be there. The air felt stale, too, as if it hadn't been disturbed for a while in any significant way. Lieber said that the *La Roca* housekeeper showed up everyday. That was her job. But there wasn't much for her to do. The bed was neat and unused and nothing was disturbed from the day before.

Standing there, I thought it through as best I could with the information I had. There were several possible explanations for Le Doux's disappearance. Sterling was tougher to figure.

Maybe she suddenly got the urge to pack up and go someplace where she didn't want to be found? But why would she do that now? The movie was important to her. It was the potential career maker she desperately needed. She told me that herself. Still, given her history of eccentric behavior and how emotionally fragile she seemed, anything was possible.

Maybe there was an emergency of some kind and she had to take care of it? It happens. But if so, why didn't she let anyone know of her whereabouts?

The third option was by far the worst. Was she taken against her will? If so, by who, to where, and what for? As far as I knew, there was no call or ransom demand.

What about her ex-husband, the dynamic Elmer Kearns? Was he involved in this? Despite what she said about him, he'd be top of my list.

I had no idea what LeDoux packed when she came to Cabo, but knowing her my guess was that she didn't travel light.

From the living room, I went into the master bedroom, and then the master bath. Particularly if it's a long trip, women often travel with a variety of lotions, unguents, creams and other unidentifiable goo that are baffling and mysterious to most men, including me. I wanted to check the bathroom to see if anything seemed to be missing.

I saw no obvious empty spaces among the various jars, bottles and tubes arrayed along the bathroom counter. There were no sticky rings where something was removed, although the La Roca staff probably would have cleaned that up. To me, it looked like LeDoux could come back any minute and have a complete lineup of whatever the hell I was looking at.

Remembering a case years ago when I recovered a missing half-million dollar diamond ring hidden in a icky jar of whatever it was, I dipped my fingers into every container. I don't know what I expected to find, but I didn't find it. The only thing I got out of it was oily fingers.

Judging by the contents of her medicine cabinet, Rio LeDoux had trouble sleeping and used everything from heavy-duty sleeping pills to over-the-counter sleep aids to put her out. In fact there were quite a few potent drugs in the cabinet. It was practically a pharmacopeia, drugs prescribed by at least five different physicians. It was hard to tell, but nothing seemed missing. No obvious empty spots in the line up.

I turned to her closet, or closets, in this case, all of which were crammed full. It looked like she could stay in Cabo for weeks and not wear the same thing twice. Among her hanging tops, there was just one empty hanger. Assuming that she didn't leave stark naked, the top she wore the day she disappeared probably came from that hanger. Dresses and skirts were all neatly in place. Nothing seemed to be missing. There was no obvious disarray like she was in a hurry, jerked a few things off their hangers and left them askew. Her shorts were neatly folded in a drawer, but it was impossible to tell if any were missing. I checked her shoes and found an empty spot on the La Roca-supplied shoe rack on the floor of the closet. Significant, I thought. Except for day trips, I have rarely known anyone to travel with only one pair of shoes. A complete set of luggage was still there, too, including an overnight bag.

Put it altogether, and I'd guess she left with only what she had on. I didn't see a purse anywhere. Nor did I find money and credit cards.

Rummaging through the drawers in the dressing room, I discovered many things that, while interesting, did me no good. Her bras were an impressive 34 DD. I've seen shoestrings that had more material than most of her panties. I also found several ounces of marijuana in a plastic baggie. There were no other drugs, which surprised me a little.

She was not a reader, which didn't surprise me at all. There were no books, no magazines, and no e-reader, although she could have taken it with her. A well-used copy of the movie script was on her bedside table. It was interesting that she didn't take the script with her. Most actors and actresses I'd known keep it close at hand during a shoot.

An Apple laptop was on the desk in the master bedroom. I decided to save that for last.

A check of my watch showed that I was okay with time.

I used the bracelet to get into the panic room; nothing there except dust bunnies. Housekeeping obviously didn't know about it.

Next I looked into the typical places where people hide things, usually places they've read about or seen in movies. I looked behind the toilet tank and in the toilet tank. I flipped the mattress off the bed, examined it on both sides, and was careful to put it back the way I found it. I didn't want the housekeeper getting suspicious, although the housekeeper probably didn't give a damn. I looked behind and underneath furniture and turned all the cushions. I checked the refrigerator and freezer combination and discovered that LeDoux liked her vodka really cold. I checked the chandelier in the living room, all the light fixtures, and, with my handy Swiss army knife, unscrewed all the plates on the electrical outlets and looked inside. I did the same with the air vents, on the walls, ceiling, and floor. In the movies, air vents are a favorite spot to hide things or escape through. In real life, not so much.

I returned to the closets and drawers and checked every pocket in every item of clothing.

Sorting through her dirty clothes, I found a business card in a blouse pocket. It was a heavy white card with embossed gold lettering. The information was minimal. It said Eros in big letters. That's all. There was no name, phone number, email or address. Not what I'd call informative.

In a search like this one, the trash can sometimes be revealing. But thanks to the damned efficiency of the *La Roca* staff, there was no trash.

By now, the atmosphere was oppressive. The situation weighed on me while I did a lot and found not much. The air seemed heavier and warmer than when I started. It wasn't, but I was still sweating up a reservoir. With my anxiety growing, I took a moment to calm down and took several deep breaths.

Now for a look at her computer.

I didn't have time to try to crack her password. I was no good at that stuff anyway. I'd leave it to Anthony, if it came to that. I *was* able to look through her documents, favorite places, and contact list.

The documents were easy. There were only three. One was a copy of the script she was shooting in Cabo, along with what looked like two other scripts. They weren't dated and the titles were not familiar, so I didn't know whether they were old scripts or something she might be considering. Based on everything I heard, she wasn't getting a lot of offers.

Finding so few documents struck me as terribly lonely. Not a single human or non-business touch there.

Her list of favorite places on the Internet didn't tell me anything either, certainly nothing that jumped out at me. Judging from a couple of the sites, she had a definite kinky side, which was not exactly a startling revelation.

I recognized a few of the names and places on her long contact list, including mine.

I printed copies of the favorite places and contact lists and stuffed them in my pocket. I'd take a more detailed look later, when I had more time.

Remembering the card I found, I took a moment and Googled Eros on LeDoux's computer. Most of what came up either had to do with a ridiculously expensive perfume that promised seduction galore or the Greek god of love, whose Roman counterpart, I learned, was Cupid.

Scrolling down, I found something interesting on the third page. It wasn't much, but it was obvious that LeDoux, or someone using her computer, had been there before, because the color of the lettering was different.

I wouldn't call it a website because it didn't have the usual website information. It barely had any information at all. All it said was "Eros" and beneath that the words "Your pleasure is our business," which, as slogans go, will get anybody's attention. There was a list of cities, too, including Los Angeles, San Francisco, New York, Boston, Miami, London, Paris, Athens, Bangkok, Hong Kong, Macao, Istanbul, Mexico City, and Rio. The bottom line said, "By invitation only."

Cabo San Lucas was one of the cities on the list.

What the hell was Eros? It wasn't a question I could answer right away. I'd been inside for nearly an hour. Lieber was probably having a nervous breakdown. Time to go.

As we agreed earlier, I texted Lieber that I was finished, waited thirty seconds, went outside and started walking toward the lobby, doing nothing to call attention to myself. He picked me up before I'd gone twenty yards.

"About goddamn time," he grumbled as we sped away on the electric cart.

When I didn't say anything, he gave me a look out of the corner of his eye.

"Well, EC, find anything?"

"Damned if I know," I said.

Chapter Thirty-Three

Ninety minutes later, courtesy of the filched card key that I promised to return to Rosa, I entered Sterling's place at *El Grande Cabo*.

This time, my search didn't take as long. With a combined living and dining area, plus one bedroom and one bath, Sterling's quarters were a lot smaller than LeDoux's and, from clothes to other goodies, there wasn't as much to go through. There was so little of everything that once again it was impossible to tell what if anything might be missing.

My search revealed that Sterling had expensive taste, right down to his silk boxer shorts, which didn't surprise me. There were no drugs, or a weapon, or anything remotely suspicious, except perhaps some heavy prescription drugs to combat anxiety. Since I didn't know what I was looking for, I wasn't sure that I'd know it if I found it.

The computer I saw him working on the day I met him was nowhere in sight, which didn't surprise me either. Sterling seemed like a guy who would never go anywhere without it, assuming he had a choice. Its absence did indicate that he left voluntarily.

The bathroom revealed that everything you'd take for even a brief overnight trip was still there, including toothpaste, toothbrush, razor, shaving cream and deodorant, just like at LeDoux's place. I didn't know if that was significant because they could buy it anywhere, although most people would take such things with them.

A Louis Vuitton rolling suitcase was on the floor in the closet. When I moved it, I discovered that the housekeepers here weren't as efficient as the housekeepers at *La Roca*. Dust had gathered on the floor under the suitcase, which told me that it hadn't been moved in a while. It's possible that Sterling had another one and took it with him. But judging by the minimal possessions, he had no need for two bags, unless he had a separate carry-on. That was one of the many things I didn't know.

After repeating my search of everything from air vents to toilet tanks, I opened the middle desk drawer in the bedroom and saw an array of business cards. I took them out and shuffled through. They were mostly local restaurants, plus several business and personal cards, most of them from Cabo San Lucas. Some of the people and places I knew, some I didn't.

Including one that said Eros, identical to the card I found at LeDoux's place.

Was this an actual clue, a nugget of information that I could move on? I was almost lightheaded with pleasure.

But what the hell was Eros?

Chapter Thirty-Four

I let myself out and walked to the underground garage to recover my car.

Once I was out in the open where I could get reception, I called Valencia.

"*Hola, jefe*," I said. "Ever hear of something called Eros?"

"Why do you want to know?"

"I'm detecting," I said. "The name came up, it's local, or it has a branch here, and I don't have a clue what it is."

"Does this have anything to do with the movie people?"

It was a reasonable question since virtually everything in Valencia's life lately had to do with the movie. I dodged it anyway.

"I'll answer your question if you'll answer mine."

"How good of you to make that concession," he said. "Where are you?"

"On the road, not far from *El Grande Cabo*."

"Can you come in?"

"Sure," I said. "How about now?"

"Now is perfect."

"I'm on the way."

* * *

The Cabo San Lucas police station was a nondescript cinder block building on an unpaved side street a few blocks away from where the tourists flock in pursuit of good times. Centrally located, but not shocking to visitors.

I parked in one of the marked spots in front of the one-story building. The overweight cop at the desk waved me through to Valencia's office down the hall. I wondered if the desk duty made him overweight or he was overweight so he got desk duty. Either way, it was an ideal combination of man and mission.

The chief's office was small but functional. Valencia only spent as much time there as he had to. There was nothing on the gray metal desk but a telephone, a legal pad, a lap top computer, and a Mont Blanc pen. There were two chairs in front of the desk and a gray metal filing cabinet in the corner, with a coffee maker on top that was about half full.

Valencia was looking at something on the computer. I knocked on the door jam and he waved me in. When I sat down, he typed something, sent it, closed the computer and asked if I wanted coffee. When I said no, he rose to pour himself a cup, adding his usual five pounds of sweetener and cream. It was as if he didn't drink coffee; he drank the stuff that he put in the coffee.

"Why do you want to know about Eros?" he asked, resuming his position in his chair.

I wasn't prepared to tell him, exactly, so I dodged like I did earlier: The truth, but not the whole truth.

"The name came up when I was doing some poking around for a client," I replied. "Whatever Eros is, it seems to be all over the world, including here in Cabo, but I've never heard of it. It probably has nothing to do with what I'm working on, but I won't know that until I find out what it is."

"How did you come across it during this 'poking around' of yours?"

This time, I saw no reason not to tell him.

"I found a card, that's all. No dead bodies riddled with bullets or whispered confessions. The card had so little information that I went on the Internet to check it out and was fascinated by how little was revealed there, too," I explained. "It's as if Eros calls attention to itself by not calling attention to itself. For my purposes, it may be something or it may be nothing, probably the latter. For all I know, it sells Love Potion Number Nine by mail order."

Valencia took a sip of his awful coffee.

"And now you've *really* got me curious." I pushed a little to see how he reacted. "With all the questions, you're acting like it's a big deal."

Valencia leaned back in his chair and put his feet up on his desk, cradling his coffee on his chest with both hands.

"At the risk of setting your curiosity on fire, I'll ask you one more time," he said. "Does this have anything to do with Rio LeDoux, the movie, or anyone associated with it?"

So far, I was getting nowhere. Neither was he. He didn't respond to my questions, and I didn't respond to his. It was like trying to dance to atonal music.

"You *do* know that I was fired, don't you?" I asked, offering a non-answer answer. "I am no longer in her employ, or that of Alton Sterling." At least that part was true.

"That was obvious after your adventure at the restaurant and the public statements that followed, all of which managed to hang it around your neck." He offered a tight little smile. "By the way, *Los Barrilas* has become quite a tourist attraction."

"Maybe I'll get a free meal out of it," I said.

We looked at each other. Valencia knew that I wasn't telling him the truth, at least not all of it. Being a cop, he was used to that. He seemed to make a decision, taking his feet off the desk and sitting up straight in his chair.

"For lack of a better way to put it, Eros is a high-class sex club," he said. "As you noticed, it has many locations around the world."

"Where is it here?"

I was surprised when he told me. It was smack in the middle of downtown Cabo, not far from Cabo Wabo. I'd passed by countless times without a clue what I was passing by.

"They *do* keep a low profile," Valencia said. "It is exclusive and upscale. There is a large fee to join, plus a substantial daily rate when a member uses the club. Members can stay for as long as they wish. You cannot be considered for membership without a recommendation from a current member, a sponsorship, I suppose you would call it. As I understand it, even that is no guarantee of acceptance."

He smiled again. "I suppose it keeps out the riff raff."

"How much to join?"

"I believe it is one hundred thousand dollars to join. The daily rate depends on the level of, ah, service required."

Once he opened up, Valencia apparently figured that he might as well go all the way.

"It's clean, comfortable for its members, and it makes no trouble," he said. "Eros takes care of its own problems. The occasionally unruly member probably is the worst of it. If everything in Cabo was run the way it is, there would not be much need for the *policia*. In four years, there has not been a single complaint. Three times I have inquired about something and the answer was prompt, complete and cooperative, all without divulging the names of their clients."

"So basically this place deals in prostitution," I said.

"Close, but a bit simplistic. High-class women - and men - who are well trained in everything from sex to the social graces are brought in from elsewhere. It does not discriminate, except that it hires no one off the street. These, ah, *employees,* if that's what they are, seem to be well cared for. They can leave at any time, but the truth is that in their business Eros is as good as it gets. It deals in privacy, absolute privacy, for its members. Say a couple wants to, ah, enliven their relationship, or perhaps experiment a bit. Or a single man or woman wants companionship for few days without entanglements or the trouble of finding it themselves. Or a gay man or woman does not want it known that they are gay and can't afford to risk discovery at home. At any of its locations, Eros is the place to go if you can afford it, which, of course, most cannot. Anonymity is guaranteed and I have never known them to violate it. I understand that no one - neither employee nor member - does anything against their will and yet virtually anything goes, except for hard drugs, as I understand it. Members can stay for a night, a week, or a month. Transactions are in cash, so there is no embarrassing record that may come to light later during, say, divorce proceedings or a review of corporate expenses."

"And you don't care?"

"Not so far. What people do in their private lives is not my concern as long as they don't violate the law. And it's better than having squadrons of prostitutes patrolling the streets and the bars, or pretending to run massage parlors. We do have some of that, as you know, but not much and certainly not high profile. The people who are drawn to Eros spend a great deal of money here, and that is much appreciated. In my experience, it is as close to a victimless operation as is possible in the real world."

"Can I get in?"

Valencia smiled again. "Why? Are you lonely?"

"But not rich. Can I talk to whoever is in charge?"

Valencia thought about it.

"I can put you in contact," he said. "But unless some law has been broken, whether or not he talks to you is up to him."

"Who is he?"

"I will tell you that if he agrees to talk."

Valencia stared, his dark eyes glittering.

"Now stop evading my questions. *Has* some law been violated? What are you up to?"

"I honestly don't know," I said. "Like I told you earlier, so far it's just the name Eros on a card that I'm checking out. It may lead nowhere, it may lead somewhere. Right now, there's no way to tell. And I can't name names. If I didn't have my own confidentiality issues I'd tell you."

"I doubt it," he said.

Chapter Thirty-Five

Valencia didn't press me on it. He told me to step outside and wait in the hall while he contacted Eros. A couple of minutes later, he called me back in.

"You can go over there now," Valencia said. "I vouched for you and he's waiting."

"You vouched for me?"

Valencia smiled. "All right, I lied and said you were someone to be trusted."

"How did he take all your vouching?" I asked. "Will he really talk to me?"

"He took it well enough. Within reason, I have always found him to be cooperative. If he can't or won't help you, he will say so and not pretend otherwise. His name, by the way, is Alonzo Zamora."

Eros was just a few blocks away so I left the Mustang parked in front of the police station and walked. When I got to where it should be there was no identification of any kind, not even an address; no sign that anything there or nearby housed the upscale sexual Disneyland that Valencia described.

At what I thought might be the right place, I pushed a doorbell beside a door painted bright blue. A small security camera just above the door moved silently, adjusting for my height. It probably took a photo, too. I was being checked out. From everything Valencia told me, I wasn't surprised.

A partition about head high opened in the middle of the door. A hairy face peered out at me.

"*Si*, what do you want?"

"Ethan Cruickshank to see Alonzo Zamora," I said. "He's expecting me."

The dark eyes that went with the hairy face looked left and right, presumably trying to see if I was alone. I could tell that vision from inside was restricted by the small size of the opening. It was a weak point in security, maybe something to be remembered, though I had no idea why.

"There is no one else with you?" Hairy Face asked.

"There is no one else with me," I said.

The partition snapped shut and the door opened.

I went inside.

* * *

With a couple of plush leather couches, several healthy looking potted plants, and an expensive waterfall feature dominating one wall, the Eros reception area resembled something you'd find at an upscale boutique hotel, but without the check-in counter. A young woman sat behind a desk facing the door. She looked up from the laptop on the desk, Hairy Face nodded; she nodded back and returned to her work. He was a hulking brute of a man, a couple of inches taller than my six feet, two inches and weighing at least 250 pounds. I followed him past the woman at the desk and down a lushly carpeted hallway. The air was cool, but with no hint that air conditioning worked hard somewhere. There was no sound at all, from inside or out. The soundproofing was exquisite.

After passing several doors, we stopped at one. Hairy Face rapped twice, opened it and we walked in. The door hissed shut behind us--heavy, expensive and expertly balanced.

We were in what looked like another reception area, although smaller; this one leading to what I suspected was an inner office behind the closed door on one wall. The expensively furnished room included another desk with another young woman behind it. Like the first one, she was attractive, with dark hair cut short; young and crisply professional. And like the first woman, she smiled and nodded at Hairy Face, although he didn't acknowledge it. Without bothering to knock, he opened the door and motioned me into the inner office, following me as I passed.

It was one of the most extraordinary sights I have ever seen. For a moment, I couldn't see anything else. The desk was big, but its massive size wasn't what held the eye. It was the material. Unbelievable as it seemed, the desk appeared to be carved or sculpted from a single piece of jade, an incredible creation of green that seemed to glow from within, somehow creating its own light. The man sitting behind it rose from a maroon leather chair that would have been suitable for the president of a very large and prosperous country and offered his hand across the vast expanse of green.

"Alonzo Zamora," he said.

"Ethan Cruickshank."

"Please, take a seat."

I sat in one of the chairs facing the remarkable desk.

"Would you like coffee or some other refreshment?"

When I declined, Zamora turned to Hairy Face.

"Thank you, Duncan," he said. "On your way out, please tell Dolores that we are not to be disturbed."

With a final glance at me – neutral, but verging on hostility – Hairy Face left the way we came.

There was a popular television commercial for Dos Equis beer featuring a character that it called "the most interesting man in the world." Alonzo Zamora could have been that man. Beneath a deep tan he looked like he might be in his mid-to-late fifties, with hair and thick beard gone to salt and pepper. His face was weathered in a way that made it interesting without seeming worn, and his voice was warm and full of experience, as if he'd seen and done things that you could only dream about and enjoyed every second of it.

"This is a beautiful desk." I ran my hand along the jade's cool edge. "The word beautiful really doesn't do it justice. I've never seen anything like it."

"Thank you," he said. "I am told that it is unique. It was a present from a grateful member several years ago."

"Your members are more grateful than my clients."

Zamora smiled, more to acknowledge my attempt at humor than my success at it.

I waved my hand to take in the rest of the opulent surroundings. The paintings on the walls looked like originals. They were mostly seascapes and very well done.

"And all of this, here and on the way in, is not what I expected."

Zamora nodded, locking his fingers beneath his chin.

"First time visitors almost always say that. They seemed shocked that we are professional, businesslike and don't bother to conceal our considerable success. But ask yourself; how else could we do what we do in the way we do it other than to be professional and businesslike? As to the décor, most of it is to my taste. All of it actually. I spend much time here and I want to be comfortable with my surroundings."

Zamora placed his hands flat on his desk, a signal that it was time to end the small talk.

"And now, what may I do for you, *Senor* Cruickshank?"

There was a slight accent, but it seemed an accent of the world, other than a specific place. The kind of accent that, no matter where you heard it, you were sure that came from somewhere else.

"How much did Valencia tell you?"

"That you wanted to see me and ask some questions pertaining to a client of yours. He offered his assurance that you would not come here to waste my time or to satisfy some idle curiosity. He said that you are a man to be taken seriously and very good at what you do."

"I'm looking for someone," I said.

"Aren't we all?" he said. "Why come to see me about it?"

I explained that I was a private detective – which he already knew – and how I found two Eros cards during a routine search on behalf of my client. I did not say who hired me, who I was looking for, or where I found the cards.

With a shrug, he said, "Our cards turn up in many places all over the world."

"I'm sure that's true, but I am only concerned about this part of the world," I said. "Someone is missing and I've been hired to find them. I'm just following up without knowing if it leads anywhere. It's part of what I do."

"And do you think the cards indicate that we have something to do with it?"

"Not necessarily. There are many possibilities, some probably peripheral, if they're connected at all, and others more to the point. Perhaps the person I'm looking for is or was a member? If not, perhaps they accompanied another member here or even applied for membership themself? Perhaps someone employed here might have heard something or has an idea where the person I'm looking for might be?"

Zamora seemed to be paying close attention, nodding as I spoke. While he might be faking it, at least he didn't dismiss me out of hand.

"You see, there are times when I don't know exactly what it is I'm looking for," I said. "I follow what information I find and see where it takes me. Sometimes it doesn't take me anywhere. But sometimes it helps point me in the right direction."

Zamora thought it over, idly fiddling with a heavy silver letter opener on the desk.

"As you say, there are many possibilities," he said. "For example, what if this person is not missing, at least not in the way you mean? What if it's a false alarm, or she does not wish to be found? Such things do happen. What will you do then?"

There it was.

Alonzo Zamora just made a mistake. I didn't mention the gender of the person I was looking for; he did. I don't think he realized what he'd done and I didn't want to alert him, so I kept talking as if I didn't notice the blunder.

"I try not to do anything against anybody's will, especially my own," I said. "I'm usually not in the returning business. I'm in the finding business. What happens when I find this person isn't up to me."

"You said 'when' you find them. Are you truly that confident?"

"I am that confident."

Neither of us wanted to take the next step.

Until I did.

"The name of the person I'm looking for is Rio LeDoux."

Zamora was good, but not quite good enough. When I said her name his eyes widened slightly. Poker players call it a tell. He instantly recovered and probably wasn't even aware of it. But combined with his earlier mistake it was more than enough. Alonzo Zamora knew something, maybe a lot of something.

"I know of this famous actress, of course, and naturally everyone in *Los Cabos* knows about the movie," he said "I also heard about what happened at a restaurant a few nights ago. I must say, I thought that you were, ah, what is the word?"

"Fired?"

An amused expression crossed his face. "I was searching for a more tactful way to express it, but yes, I thought you were fired. If she is no longer your client, then who is?"

"Aside from concerns for her safety, the movie is important. Reputations are at stake, as are hundreds of millions of dollars. Everyone involved from the studio president down to catering wants to make it a success for obvious reasons. All of these people would like to know Rio LeDoux's whereabouts, or at least what happened to her. They want to know if she is safe, and when or if she'll return. Beyond that, I cannot tell you more."

"So has Rio LeDoux ever been here?" I decided to hold Sterling's name back for now. "Have you seen her, or know anyone who has? It's possible that she might have used different name. With all the publicity, I'm sure that you know what she looks like. If not, I have a photo."

I let my eyes roam around the room, trying to be tactful while still learning as much as possible.

"In an odd way, I don't really know where *here* is," I said. "Valencia explained what Eros does, the service it provides. But where do your, um, activities transpire?"

Transpire? Where did I get that one?

Zamora opened his arms and raised them to his shoulders. There was something proud and even proprietary in the gesture.

"They *transpire*, as you say, all around us. You might be surprised to learn that we own this entire square block and our facility goes down two more levels. The storefronts on the street level are perfectly legitimate, the better to avoid calling unwanted attention to ourselves. Our membership is exclusive. We don't want curious people walking in off the street. The shops and restaurants we own make a welcome profit. But the true pleasures we provide are above us, below us, on all sides, and at all times, even as you and I sit here."

Zamora seemed to be captured by an almost evangelical fervor. Why not? There are worse things to be passionate about.

"Take a moment, Mister Cruickshank. Step outside of yourself and concentrate. You can feel it, can't you? I know you can. Sooner or later, everyone does."

It probably was only the power of suggestion, but I could swear at that moment there *was* something. It was like a pleasing but unfamiliar scent or an emotion that couldn't be described. It had power, substance, and, like he said, I could feel it around us.

Zamora broke the strange mood. "But I am afraid that I cannot help you. I am sorry to disappoint, but what you ask is impossible."

I wasn't really disappointed, though I tried to look like it. I would have been surprised if he'd offered to help. I hardly expected him to say, "Oh, yes, Rio LeDoux is in room thirty four with a supply of peanut butter and bowling balls, plus a goat and three *hombres* named Jose, Lars, and Pierre."

"You must understand that privacy, absolute privacy, is at the heart of what we offer," he explained. "For us to violate it for any reason is simply impossible, even if there is no consequence to us. You obviously are a man of the world and I'm sure you can see it from our perspective. After all, I believe that you call yourself a *private* detective."

"All right, I understand," I said agreeably. "But what if I talk to your employees? Purely informational and anonymous. I promise that nothing will come of it except, perhaps, to give me some direction. No one else will ever know that we talked."

I was sure that Zamora would turn that down, too. He did not disappoint me.

"I am sorry, but I cannot allow that either," he said, expressing regret he obviously did not feel. "And, of course, I'm sure you expected me to say that, although I know that you had to try. We seem to have come to an impasse. You want what I cannot provide under any circumstances."

Zamora rose to his feet, offering his hand again.

"I apologize for being so little help and I wish you well in your search." He nodded toward the door. "Duncan will show you out."

Zamora pressed a button on the jade desk and Hairy Face entered the room within a nano second. He was obviously waiting just outside the door in case I tried anything with his boss. I didn't see a security camera in the office but that doesn't mean there wasn't one. It probably was set up for sound, too.

Looking properly disappointed, I shook Zamora's hand and was quickly escorted to the front door by Hairy Face.

Out on the street, I smiled at the camera and walked away, knowing a lot more than I did when I got here.

Chapter Thirty-Six

I recovered the Mustang from the *policia* station, drove home and made a couple of calls: One to Heenan to see if he made any more progress. The other call went to Anthony. It was time to turn him loose on Sterling and his finances.

There was some personal business to take care of, too. After lurking out in the Pacific for a while, Hurricane Isabel had become a huge and potentially lethal storm. On course to hit Cabo San Lucas within the next twenty-four to thirty-six hours, it was taking its sweet time about it, dawdling while it gained strength and gradually moved closer to land. The storm's erratic behavior was like no hurricane in memory. By the time it made landfall, Isabel could easily exceed two hundred miles an hour, the most powerful storm to hit Cabo in decades.

My house was equipped with storm shutters at all the windows and glass doors and I spent a couple of hours lowering and fastening each one so that it would stay down tight no matter what.

Then I called Miguel Ortiz, who I sometimes employed as a gardener and landscaper, and asked him to send someone over to take care of the coconut palms on the property. High wind can turn the innocent coconut into a deadly projectile. A ten-pound coconut propelled by hurricane winds has the power and weight to kill. It can cause a lot of property damage, too. The young man Ortiz sent out for the job spent most of the rest of the day shinnying up every palm tree on the property and hacking down bunches of coconuts with a machete. By the time he finished, the insides of his thighs looked like raw meat and his arms must have felt like strands of spaghetti.

Elsewhere in the world, there probably was some kind of mechanized apparatus that accomplished the same thing with much less labor and time. But in Mexico, labor is almost always cheaper than machinery. When the weary tree climber finished and piled the coconuts in his pickup truck to be hauled away, I gave him a five hundred peso bonus, in addition to whatever Miguel paid him.

I have been through hurricanes in different part of the world and they do not terrify me. It helps that, unlike, say, earthquakes and tornadoes, you do get a lot of warning. Unless you live in a trailer park, shabbily constructed housing, or an old building that's not up to modern construction standards, you should come through a hurricane all right. That's unless you do something stupid, which means about half the population is in jeopardy when a hurricane hits anywhere in the world. Stupidity knows no national boundaries. It's amazing how many tourists go out to the beach and see the big waves, which can turn out to be the last thing they ever see. There are occasional exceptions to my stupid-substandard-housing-trailer-park rule, like Hurricane Katrina and New Orleans. But that astonishing disaster had more to do with government and engineering incompetence piled up over many years.

With the pre-hurricane work done, I checked my inventory: several cases of bottled water, enough food canned and otherwise to last at least a week, and a couple of oil lamps I could use when the power went out, which it was guaranteed to do in Cabo. Cell phone service probably would go out, too.

By the time I was ready for Hurricane Isabel, Heenan and Anthony got back to me.

They both reported the same thing: just before Alton Sterling disappeared, he withdrew more than $75,000 from his personal bank account.

"He made the withdrawal at his bank in Century City, though that doesn't mean he's still in the area," explained Heenan, who was the first to call. "My guess is that he isn't. Nobody I contacted has heard from him or about him. From everything I've been able to find, the withdrawal pretty much taps him out. I don't think he's got a secret stash in the Cayman Islands, or anything"

"Thanks, Eddie," I said. "Anything on Kearns?"

"I was getting to that."

"What?"

"He's dead."

"What? How? What happened?"

"It looks like a suicide," he replied. "They found his body at Venice Beach yesterday morning. Apparently he drove to the beach sometime late the night before, parked his car, walked out on the beach, sat down and drank about a quarter of the bottle of tequila he brought with him, probably to work up the courage. Then he stuck a forty five in his mouth and blew the top of his head off."

"Did he leave a note?" I asked.

"The cops didn't find any," Heenan replied. "And now you know as much about it as I do."

After that, there was nothing more to say.

I was diverted from thoughts of Kearns blowing his brains out on a dark Southern California beach when Anthony called. In his usual longwinded way, he had more detail.

"After withdrawing seventy five thousand four hundred and thirty six dollars, which left fourteen dollars in his account, Sterling crossed the border into Mexico at Tecate, east of San Diego. He was driving a hired vehicle, a Jeep Cherokee, which he picked up in Los Angeles. I'm sorry to report that there is no sign of him since then. His name does not appear at any hotels or resorts. He bought no airline tickets and there are no credit card charges, not even for petrol. Nothing at all so far. I would say that Sterling is deliberately keeping the lowest possible profile by living on what he has in his pocket, which, unless he liquidates some property, and that seems unlikely since he is mortgaged to his eyeballs, is all he has."

It was an easy three-day drive from the border to Cabo San Lucas, two days if you pushed a little. If Sterling was coming this way, he was more than likely here by now.

"One more thing, Anthony," I asked. "Do you have a Cabo address for a man named Alonzo Zamora?"

I spelled the name and he said that he'd call back as soon as he had the information. His search took all of four minutes; it was the same address as Eros.

"Are you sure that's not just a mail drop, or something?" I asked. "He really lives there?"

Anthony harrumphed a bit, pretending to be offended. "Ethan, old boy, if I wasn't sure I wouldn't present the information as fact. That address is Zamora's living quarters, although he does have a separate mail drop at a facility in a nearby shopping mall."

Before I ended the call, Anthony offered a warning.

"Ethan, as usual, I don't know what all this is leading to, but, whatever you might be planning in the next few days, I advise you be very careful of that hurricane," he said. "It looks particularly mean and the potential for devastation is high, very high. I do hope your area is ready for it. Mexico is not known for its ability to withstand this kind of thing with any ease."

He laughed when I told him that careful was my middle name. He knew better.

So Alonzo Zamora lived at Eros. That's one way to take your work home with you. From the way he described it, the place was certainly big enough. From what I saw, there was no doubt he lived well too. If it was open twenty-four hours a day, seven days a week, as it seemed to be, I wouldn't be surprised if key members of the staff lived there, too, including my good friend Duncan. If he wanted to, that man could be quite an obstacle.

How did Kearns' suicide fit into the puzzle? Or did it? The timing didn't eliminate him from involvement in LeDoux's disappearance, although Anthony confirmed that there was no record of his returning to Mexico after Valencia put him on a plane to the United States, just as there was no record of LeDoux leaving Mexico for the United States or anywhere else. After my stunt with the gun at the Hotel Cortez, to get back into Mexico Kearns would have needed a false passport. That was always possible, but somehow I doubted it.

Instinct told me that Kearns had nothing to do with any of what I was working on. Over the years, I've learned to trust instinct. I've met too many guys like Kearns. He was a sad wreck of a man who couldn't handle life anymore, a tough guy wannabe who probably looked in the mirror one day, saw a man who failed at everything he did and hated what he saw. He was in love with a woman he could never have, at least not in the way he wanted. Our only meeting was not exactly friendly, but I felt sorry for him. I doubt that he would have returned the feeling.

My thoughts turned to Eros. In addition to Zamora and the "staff" it took to provide the kind of service I could only imagine, I wondered who else might be there. Throw in a few frolicsome "members" and Eros might have quite a crowd.

Who knows, it probably wouldn't be a bad place to ride out a hurricane?

Or to hide out, for some reason.

Chapter Thirty-Seven

The next morning, the forecast for Hurricane Isabel was that she would make landfall by early afternoon, packing a hell of a punch. The wind already blew high, the rain poured, and everyone in the Los Cabos area was warned to stay off the streets. If the wind and rain didn't get them, the tidal surge and flooding might. Being told to stay indoors wouldn't make the tourists happy, but they wouldn't like getting blown halfway to South America either.

As I drank coffee and watched the news, something gnawed at my subconscious like a rabid wolverine. Somewhere there was a detail I had overlooked or something that didn't fit that I should be able to see.

Whatever it was, I couldn't bring it into focus. I knew from experience that straining over it wouldn't help. If I just let it go it might come to me like one of those moments when you wake up in the middle of the night and go "Aha!" It can be embarrassing if you're not alone.

I decided to check in with Odermeyer, who was, after all, my client. Fortunately, cell service wasn't out yet. He seemed relieved to hear from me. I was surprised when he said that most of the movie people decided to ride out the hurricane in Cabo San Lucas. He explained that anyone who went back to Southern California would only have to turn around and come back in a few days anyway. The crew had dismantled and stored anything that the hurricane might damage and it wouldn't take long to put the whole thing back together and get back to work.

As far as Odermeyer knew, nobody had heard from either LeDoux or Sterling. In a way, the hurricane's imminent arrival was a lucky break because it diverted attention from the actress' absence. Apparently nobody missed Sterling yet because he wasn't part of the movie-making apparatus. But if LeDoux didn't turn up once the hurricane passed and shooting began again, Odermeyer couldn't keep a lid on it any longer.

I told him that I was making progress but it was too soon to say anything for sure. He found that irritating and got a little testy with me. I didn't blame him. He complained that either I was making progress or I wasn't, but either way he had a right to know what was going on. I agreed that he did indeed have that right, but I still didn't tell him anything. He didn't like that either.

I didn't want to say anything because I wasn't sure what I had, or if I really had it. I also wanted as few people as possible to know that I was looking for LeDoux and Sterling. Some already knew, of course, but that was unavoidable and there weren't many, only Odermeyer, Zamora, Heenan, Anthony and maybe Duncan if Zamora told him. Whatever happened, I didn't want to lose the advantage of secrecy. If I told Odermeyer what I found, or what I suspected, he might blab it to someone.

I decided to take my own advice, not do anything stupid, and wait out Hurricane Isabel at home. The waves were already running as high as twenty feet, pounding the shore the way a hammer meets an anvil, and they were predicted to get bigger. The English-language TV news was putting out more wind than the storm, chattering about how virtually everything in Los Cabos would be closed for at least the next couple of days, including all the financial institutions and government offices. The financial institutions were important because even with credit cards tourists still need cash, especially if the storm knocked out communications so cards couldn't be approved for use by restaurants and shops.

Financial institutions?

As in banks?

It all started to come together. Sterling withdrew more than $75,000 in cash from his bank. Until now, I assumed that was because he wanted to keep his movements secret and knew that credit card charges could be traced. But there was something Valencia said. What was it? I closed my eyes and tried to reconstruct the conversation.

He said that Eros dealt only in cash.

Aha! My moment had come.

Chapter Thirty-Eight

Armed with that epiphany, I decided to ignore my own advice and go out in the hurricane after all. Actually, if I hurried I'd get downtown before the hurricane, although not much before.

It might be risky, but I couldn't pass it up. There was a chance that everybody I was supposed to find might be at Eros. It was short of a sure thing, but I couldn't ignore it. The hurricane even worked for me. Nobody at Eros would expect visitors. Only a crazy man would go out in a storm like this.

Out I went.

I armed myself with a Colt Python carried in a shoulder holster. An old favorite when it came to stopping power, it was big enough to bring down Mars. I also like the Python because with its six-inch barrel it looks scary as hell. At two-and-a-half pounds, it's like carrying a brick under my arm, but that's a small price to pay for intimidation. For backup, as usual I packed a little twenty-two caliber in an ankle holster.

I shrugged into a nylon windbreaker to keep off at least some of the rain and took along a Detroit Tigers baseball cap, too. I don't care much for baseball. It always puts me to sleep. But the hat was a good way to change my look, not to mention the potential for keeping my head dry.

Equipped and clad, I got in the Mustang and drove like hell for downtown Cabo.

The world was an uneasy place, with a strong sense of looming danger. The sky had a strange cast that was somewhere between gray and yellow. I could see the massive dark clouds of the hurricane swirling over the ocean as it approached. I hadn't gone far before I was reminded why it was tricky to drive in these conditions. It was a good thing that I was the only car on the road because the wind's incredible power caused me to make a couple of unscheduled lane changes. A couple of times I was afraid that it might rip off the convertible top, too.

I was already having second thoughts about my little venture, but it was too late to turn back. I was committed. Now I had to find a way to get into Eros before the hurricane creamed Cabo San Lucas. And me along with it.

Chapter Thirty-Nine

For once, parking downtown was easy to find. I was the only fool on the road.

I parked on a narrow side street where the Mustang might be shielded a little from the elements. It was all I could do to muscle the car door open against the wind. When I finally got it open it felt like the wind might rip the door off its hinges. The drops of rain were huge. Every one hit like a tiny bomb. Once I forced the car door shut I started walking. When I turned the corner, the wind bounced me along for at least twenty feet before I got my balance and anchored myself against its power. All this, and the hurricane wasn't even here yet.

Hugging the shuttered shops and restaurants, I fought my way along foot by foot. If the security camera at the Eros entrance was still working, I wanted whoever answered the door to think that I was a dumb tourist who got caught outside and desperately needed shelter. It wouldn't be much of a stretch because the longer I was out in the storm, the more I felt like exactly that.

I pounded on the blue door and rang the bell several times, making sure to keep my head down. With the baseball cap, the camera couldn't get a look at my face. When no one answered, I pounded and rang again, this time crying out for help like a desperate man, which I nearly was anyway.

Just as I was about to give up, the small partition in the door opened to reveal Duncan's hairy mug.

Still keeping my head down so he couldn't see my face, I hugged the blue door, fighting the rising wind.

"Please! Please, let me in!" I begged. "The hurricane's coming and there's no where else to go! My friends left me alone and I don't want to die out here!"

"*Stupido!*" Duncan sneered as he started to close the partition.

My fabrication didn't work. I went to plan B, drew the Python and pointed it through the partition at Duncan's big nose.

"I know that you speak English," I said, raising my head so he could see who I was. "If you don't open the door right now, I will blow your face off."

He hesitated. I could tell by his eyes that he was calculating his chances.

I cocked the Python.

That did it. He opened the door and I put my foot in so he couldn't slam it shut.

"Now raise your hands and step back."

He did, still glowering.

I kicked the door all the way open and had the Python on him before he could do anything, though that big body was ready to spring.

"Don't even think about it, *stupido*," I said. "Turn around and face the wall."

Fortunately, the young lady was no longer on duty at the desk. Eros obviously was not expecting any visitors during a hurricane.

I brought two pairs of PlastiCuffs with me for moments like this. When Duncan turned around, I put a pair on his big wrists and pushed him hard against the wall. It was like moving a safe. Then I jammed the Python barrel into the small of his back, right at the spine.

"Where's Zamora?"

When he didn't answer, I jammed harder, which forced him to straighten up against the wall.

"If you don't tell me, I will shoot you through the spine. If that doesn't kill you, you will be a cripple for the rest of your life." I spoke slowly and clearly, not sure how good Duncan's English was. "I'll find Zamora with you or without you. Without you, it will just take longer. It's your choice, big boy."

Duncan took a deep shuddering breath. "He is in his apartment, I think."

"Good choice, Duncan," I said. "You're not as dumb as you look."

I stepped back, keeping one hand on the cuffs and raising Duncan's arms behind his back, the Python ready in the other hand.

"Take me there. Remember, if you try to warn him, no matter what happens to me I will shoot you first." I jabbed him in the back again. "Move slow and keep quiet."

We slowly marched down the carpeted hallway. The position was awkward for me. Holding up Duncan's cuffed arms up behind his back with one hand was heavy going. But it was a hell of a lot more awkward for him. From that position it was impossible to make any kind of offensive move. Good.

Chapter Forty

We walked down the hall, made a turn, and went down a flight of stairs to another hall. Zamora wasn't kidding. This place seemed to go on forever.

We stopped in front of a door that looked like all the other doors.

"He is in here," Duncan said, his rumbling voice at a whisper.

"Is he alone?" I asked, whispering back.

Duncan shrugged his massive shoulders to indicate that he didn't know.

"When you come here, do you knock or call out?"

"Both," he said.

"Okay, I'll knock and you call. Tell him there's a problem with someone at the entrance, someone who asked for him by name. And remember, I understand your language so I'll know if you say anything else."

I turned Duncan to the side and knocked on the door with the butt of the Python. When Duncan didn't say anything, to remind him of his role, I kicked him hard in the calf. It nearly buckled his leg and I was rewarded with a rumbling "*Senor* Zamora" from the big man, along with the request that he was needed to take care of a problem with someone at the door who wanted in.

Zamora probably would think it strange that Duncan came to his room instead of calling, or however they communicated down here, but I didn't care. All I wanted him to do was answer the door.

I maneuvered Duncan so that he was facing the door again. When it opened, I put my back into him and shoved him through with all my strength. Off balance, he staggered into the room and knocked over

Zamora the way a bowling ball knocks over a bowling pin. With Duncan's hands behind his back he couldn't keep his balance, tripped over Zamora and went down hard himself.

Covering both men with the Python, I stepped in and shut the door behind me, facing a tangle of arms and legs.

Chapter Forty-One

"Both of you stay down!"

A glance around the living room showed that, except for the giant jade desk, the décor was similar to Zamora's office, expensively masculine and heavy on the leather.

"Is anybody else in here?"

Zamora, who had maneuvered himself into a sitting position after being run over by Duncan, shook his head.

"I don't know what you think you are doing, but you are making a big mistake," he said.

Unfortunately for Zamora, it's hard to appear threatening when you've just been knocked on your butt in the middle of your own living room.

"I'm used to it," I said.

I had a problem: Too many people. I needed Zamora to guide me through this confusing place so I could find Sterling and LeDoux, assuming they were here, and then show me how to get the hell out. But what would I do with Duncan in the meantime? I couldn't bring him along. The big guy was too dangerous.

I had an idea. It was cruel, but I didn't like Duncan anyway. It had the added advantage of putting some fear into Zamora and probably made him more cooperative.

Duncan was still on the floor, sitting up, like Zamora. I shifted the Python to my left hand. With my right, I pulled the twenty-two from my ankle holster.

And then I shot him in the knee.

The caliber was small but the gunshot was loud. Duncan screamed and clutched his knee. I took a step back, the Python in my left hand and the twenty-two in my right.

Ethan Cruickshank, gunslinger.

"You bastard!" Zamora snarled, while Duncan writhed on the carpeted floor.

I didn't say anything. We gun-slinging bastards never do. I was careful to shoot Duncan just above the knee. As much as I didn't like him, I didn't want to shatter his kneecap, just put him out of action, which was why I used the twenty-two. The Python might have blown his leg off. I doubted that he appreciated my concern.

"All right, Zamora," I said. "Get up."

He got to his feet, but slowly, bringing his venomous look with him.

"Now you're going to take me to Sterling and LeDoux," I said.

"You can't just leave him here," he protested, motioning at Duncan. "He'll bleed to death."

"No he won't," I said. "Look at him. He's barely bleeding now. He just won't go on any long hikes for a while."

It was interesting that Zamora didn't deny that Sterling and LeDoux were around here somewhere. I'd guessed right.

"He still needs a doctor," Zamora insisted.

"If you do what I tell you, he'll get one soon enough," I said. "But the longer we stand here, the longer it'll take."

Waving the twenty-two, I motioned Zamora toward the door. Reluctantly, he started moving, leaving the cursing Duncan on the floor holding his leg.

When we were out in the hallway, I slipped the twenty-two back into the ankle holster and transferred the Python to my right hand.

"You know, I can't be sure where they are," Zamora said.

"How many options are there?" I asked.

"At least two; the big room and his suite."

"What's the big room?"

"It is just what it sounds like," replied Zamora, who had regained control of himself. "Some of our members think of themselves as exhibitionists. They like a crowd, even a form of group sex, small or large. No matter whether they like to watch others, participate, or have others watch them, it makes no difference to us as long as none of the other members object."

"It sounds like an old-fashioned orgy," I said.

"We use other language but I suppose someone as crude as you are would call it that."

"What do LeDoux and Sterling usually do?"

Zamora shook his head. "There is no usually. This is the first time the actress has come here. She is Sterling's guest, a privilege that we offer one time only. For her to return to any Eros anywhere in the world, she must be a member. As for him, his tastes are, ah, varied."

"Varied? What does that mean?"

"Couples, trios, groups, same sex. Over time, he has indulged in almost everything in many of our locations. It is possible that he has difficulties."

"Difficulties?"

"A physician or psychiatrist might call it performance issues. I think that's why he keeps trying different *situations*, shall we say."

"I suppose we shall," I said. "Why doesn't he just take Viagra, or something? The sell it in every pharmacy on every street corner in Cabo."

"Pride, I suppose. I am not a psychiatrist. We do not judge or question motives here."

"Bully for you," I said.

I don't even know why I asked the question in the first place. Zamora's answer certainly was more information than I wanted.

"Which is closest, the big room or their suite?"

"The big room."

"Take me there."

I stayed behind Zamora, holding on to his belt with my left hand and keeping the Python on him with my right. I didn't know the extent of Eros' security and I wanted him close enough for cover in case we rounded a corner and ran into someone who did not wish me well.

Down the hall, when Zamora moved toward an elevator I pulled him back and told him that we were going to walk. I didn't want any surprises when the elevator door opened on either end.

At the end of the hall, we went down stairs that resembled the service stairs in a hotel, entered another hallway, and then walked what seemed like a long way, making several turns. If the big room was closest of the two possibilities, the suite must be in Connecticut.

Zamora stopped at large double doors.

"The big room?" I asked.

Zamora nodded.

For the first time, I could hear sound other than our own; the hard thumping of bass from music I no doubt hated came from behind the doors. Before Zamora led us in, I had a thought.

"I bet you have a place where you can watch what's going on in there without anyone knowing," I said "A one-way mirror, cameras, something like that. Am I right?"

"You are."

"You like to watch, too, huh? Kinky."

Zamora actually seemed offended. "It's for security, in case anyone misbehaves."

"Misbehaves? How the hell can anyone misbehave in a place like this?"

"As I told you, we have strict rules and we enforce them. You may not believe that, but it is the truth. Security is needed in case someone becomes violent in unacceptable ways, or uses drugs that we do not allow, among other transgressions. We are strict about what cannot take place and every member signs a document specifying that they will not violate our rules at the risk of lifetime expulsion. S and M are allowed within reason, but nothing here happens against an individual's will. Not at any time."

Zamora hesitated, appeared to be undecided about saying something, and then went ahead with it.

"There is one more thing. You probably will not believe me until you see for yourself, but unfortunately you can't see everyone in the big room though the mirror and cameras, at least not their faces."

Faces were all I was interested in. Even if Zamora was telling the truth, I figured it still was worth a try. I didn't want the search to take any longer or be any more disruptive than it had to. The longer I kept things quiet, the better off I'd be. Strolling through an orgy with a gun in Zamora's back would probably count as disruptive.

"We'll try the mirror and cameras first," I said. "Take me there."

Chapter Forty-Two

We turned away from the double doors, went up more service stairs and stopped at another anonymous-looking door with a "Private" sign on it. Zamora punched some numbers on the security pad next to the door, pulled it open, and we walked in.

A bank of TV monitors covered most of one wall in the cramped room. A bored-looking young man wearing jeans and a t-shirt sat in an armless chair in front of the monitors, rising in alarm when he saw that I had a gun at Zamora's back. Zamora shook his head and waved him back down to the chair.

The dozen monitors appeared to work off standard black-and-white security cameras scattered in various locations around the big room, most of them looking down. Like most security cameras, the picture quality was grainy but adequate. It was like watching a 1950s-era porn movie and about as enticing as a three-hour pitch about actuarial prudence.

As Zamora promised, the screens revealed couples, trios, small groups and larger groups. Everyone I could see was nude, partially clothed, or making progress in that direction. There seemed to be some conversation, but almost everyone was seriously committed to sex, although it didn't look like a particularly good time. I didn't see anybody who appeared to be genuinely enjoying what they were doing.

It was impossible to get a good perspective of the room through the monitors and I turned to the big window that overlooked the room on the opposite wall.

Standing beside me, Zamora anticipated my questions. I had forgotten all about him. He could have made a run for it but probably didn't want to risk ending up like Duncan.

"The cameras are concealed so that no one in the room knows they are there, although I doubt very much that it would inhibit most of our members. On the contrary, it probably would excite many of them. The room also has many mirrors. All but this one are just that, mirrors. We do not tell our members about these things, although I would not be surprised if most suspected that they exist. As I told you, this is strictly for security. We destroy all recordings after a reasonable period of time and no Eros establishment anywhere in the world has ever had a leak to the tabloids or the Internet."

The big mirror-window was well above the action and offered less detail but a better perspective of the room than the cameras. The sight resembled what might happen if you combined a painting by Heironymus Bosch and a hot weekend with Caligula & Co. The room actually looked a little cheesy. I expected more in the way of opulence. The whole thing resembled a 1970s-era disco, complete with a multi-colored flashing-lights dance floor. From what I could see, unless you're in great shape I don't recommend dancing in the nude. Too many moving parts. The surveillance room was sound proofed but I could still feel the thumping bass. A self-service bar was at one end of the room and there were curtained alcoves on the floor along the walls, although some of the curtains were open. I assumed they were for anyone who wanted a little privacy, although I couldn't imagine what anyone who wanted privacy was doing here I the first place. There was food available somewhere because I saw a much-too-hairy guy eating sushi off of a well-shaped female butt. Judging by the cloud of smoke that wafted to the ceiling, there was enough marijuana being smoked to light up all of Jamaica. There looked to be quite a bit of role-playing, too. I saw several uniformed maids in short skirts, a guy dressed as a lion tamer, including the whip, one Wonder Woman and two versions of Batman.

I estimated that there might be two hundred people in various stages of whatever they were doing, and no doubt more than that since I couldn't see everything. As Zamora warned, it was difficult to pick out individuals, or focus on any detail at all. Occasionally, I would catch a glimpse of a face, enough to know that it wasn't LeDoux or Sterling.

At this rate, I'd have to watch for the rest of the week while still keeping an eye on Zamora and the guy at the monitors, which did not appeal to me on any level.

"You were right," I admitted. "This is impossible. Neither one of us wants me to stay here for as long as it would take to make an ID. We might as well go to their suite and hope we get lucky."

I eyed at the young guy, but asked Zamora, "Does he have a telephone?"

"There is an in-house system, plus I assume he has a cell phone," he replied.

The in-house telephone was on a small desk in front of the monitors. I jerked the line out of the wall, tossed the telephone on the floor and stomped it to pieces.

I held out my hand to the young guy.

"*Dame su teléfono cellular!*" I demanded.

Frightened out of his wits by the Python, he dug into the pocket of his jeans and handed over his smart phone.

I dropped it on the floor and stomped it into little pieces, too.

I told him to turn around and braided the PlastiCuffs through the back of his chair before slipping them on his skinny wrists.

"Tell him that if he leaves this room I will shoot him just like I shot Duncan."

Even before Zamora translated, the kid nodded his head with great enthusiasm. I don't know if he understand the words, but he got the message.

Chapter Forty-Three

We left the cramped room and walked down the hall. I kept the Python pressed into Zamora's spine. Fortunately, we didn't pass anyone on the way because I was out of cuffs.

Just before we reached the end of the hall, Zamora stopped at a door.

"This is it?" I asked.

"Yes."

"Do you have a master key?"

Zamora shook his head. "I do, but everything happened so fast I didn't think to bring it."

My fault. I should have thought of that.

"Tell me, how solid is the door?"

Zamora appeared confused by the question.

"Can I kick it in?" I explained.

"I don't know," he answered. "It depends on ... I suppose so but I'm really not sure."

"Is there another way out of there?"

"No."

At least he was sure about that. I'd make a lot of noise kicking the door in but if LeDoux and Sterling were inside there was no way for them to escape, unless Zamora lied to me. I didn't want to knock or call out because surprise was my friend. And I didn't know who else might be inside. Somebody in there might be armed, or they might not, but just in case I had to assume that they were.

"Okay, stand back!"

Zamora backed up. I took a deep breath, raised my foot and kicked the door around the doorknob once, twice, three times. The door splintered and I shouldered it open the rest of the way. It was not bad construction. With cheap doors, one kick usually is enough.

I grabbed Zamora by the shoulder, pushed him through the doorway and followed him in, the Python raised and ready.

Chapter Forty-Four

We were in the living room of a suite. It could have been a middling-quality hotel almost anywhere.

So far, the whole Eros experience was a serious disappointment. I expected fantastic luxury combined with a kind of sophisticated sensual decadence that can only be imagined. What I'd seen so far resembled a lot of desperate people groping each other in the bar at a Holiday Inn on Saturday night.

The difference was the Holiday Inn didn't have Alton Sterling in it.

It was not the man I remembered standing in the middle of the room gaping at the intruders with his mouth open. His once perfectly styled hair was shaggy, tousled and dirty. He hadn't shaved in a while and the gray stubble on his face looked made him look older. His eyes were bleary and bloodshot, a sign that he was either drinking too much or not sleeping enough, maybe both. I couldn't count out drugs either. And the once-immaculate wardrobe had gone to hell. He was barefoot and looked like he hadn't bothered to change clothes recently. This was a man who either didn't care anymore or who was so focused on something that there wasn't room in his head for anything else.

"Where is she?" I said, making sure that Sterling had a good view of the Python.

I'm not sure that he even saw it as his eyes moved from me to Zamora and back again.

Finding his voice, he asked the obvious question. "What ... what is the meaning of this? What do you think you're doing? Get out of here, both of you!"

It was a weak effort. It was too late for outraged dignity and I think he knew it.

"Where is she?" I asked again, raising the Python and pointing it at Sterling.

"Stop! There's no need for that," Zamora shouted. He lifted his chin toward the other end of the living room, where a bedroom went off to one side to create an L shape. "If the actress is here, she must be over there."

"Why are you so cooperative all of a sudden?" I asked, keeping the Colt on Sterling.

"Because I want you out of here," Zamora explained. "And I see now that the only way to make that happen is to help you get what you want. So far, none of our members know you are here or what you are doing. I want to keep it that way. If it means cooperating with you, then I will cooperate for as long as necessary."

It seemed reasonable, within limits. Suddenly, we were allies, though he'd still bear watching.

The empty shell that once was Alton Sterling just stood there, as if he couldn't figure out why *he* was here, let alone these intruders.

That changed when we started toward the bedroom. Sterling jumped in front of me and shouted, "No! You can't go in there!"

Without breaking stride, I brushed him aside with one arm. He staggered and fell to his knees. It was like bullying a ninety-year-old man. It was as if there was no strength left in him at all. There was no time to feel sorry for him, even if I was inclined. There was no time for anything except to find who I'd come for and get the hell out of this place.

Chapter Forty-Five

Rio LeDoux was on the big bed. She wore a white satin strap dress that would have been slinky looking if she'd been on her feet. She was barefoot, with her right leg up and bent at the knee, her foot beside her other knee.

The room was strangely lit. It was a moment before I realized that the only illumination came from candles. They were everywhere, dozens of them. They covered the dresser and the bedside tables. There were a couple of dining room chairs beside the bed with candles on those, too. The flickering of the candles in the semi-darkness made the scene incredibly erotic.

Or it would have if not for LeDoux's makeup. It looked like it was applied by a blind man using a trowel. Bright red lipstick was smeared all around her mouth and the eye makeup, or whatever it was, was hideously packed on in widespread layers.

The effect was ghastly, even a little frightening. I stood still for a moment, not sure what I was seeing. Behind me, as he entered the room I heard Zamora gasp. Then it came to me: It looked like a shrine, a shrine gone terribly wrong.

Except for her grotesque face, LeDoux looked like a perfect marble sculpture that was expertly lighted, a scene of innocent purity combined with the massively erotic.

I stepped to the side of the bed. LeDoux's eyes were closed. She was breathing regularly and there was no sign of injury.

"Remarkable, isn't she?" Sterling was beside me, his voice a whisper. "She's perfect, the way she should always be. The way I made her. It took time, but I finally got it right."

Sterling was so edgy he was practically vibrating out of his clothes.

"You see, when the time is right, I know she will give herself to me. Once she understands, I know she will."

He knelt beside the bed, gazing at his macabre creation.

"I only want to help her become what she should always have been, perfect in every way. All these years, she wouldn't let me help her. Oh, she let me handle her business affairs, but she never understood that I was destined to do more than that. She was going to get rid of me. She didn't know I knew that, but I know her better than anyone. I didn't want to do it now, but she forced me. It was my last chance, *our* last chance. We were always meant to be. You see, I'm the only one in the world who really cares about her. She was this ... thing to them, to *all* of them, a commodity to be used and discarded. She didn't know ... she never understood her potential. It would only happen if I guided her. But only I knew that. Only I could make it come true for her. But she didn't listen to me. She never listened. She scorned me and mocked me. But that was all right. I understood. I was patient. I knew how she really felt, even if she didn't know it herself. And finally ... finally ... I had to save her because no one else could. It was all up to me. It'll be all right now ... just the two of us. We can be together now."

Something disturbed Sterling's thoughts and he left the tracks again.

"Why are you here?" Agitated, he rose to his feet, shouting and waving his arms. "Get out! Get out of here right now! You have no right to be here!"

I gave him a stiff arm in the chest with my left hand that put him on the floor one more time. He was so weak that it didn't take much of an effort.

With all the commotion, LeDoux had to be drugged or she'd be awake by now.

"Sterling, what did you give her to make her like this?"

Still on the floor, he glared at me with hate in his eyes but didn't answer.

"I suspect that it might be Rohypnol," Zamora said. "It and other drugs like it are better known as 'roofies,' the date-rape drug. It's one of the drugs we don't permit here."

"I know what roofies are." I was tired of the pretension that Zamora and Eros were engaged in some kind of higher calling for the good of mankind. "And if you're right, then the security in this dump sucks."

"If they are administered properly roofies are difficult to detect," he said, ignoring the insult. "She could be ambulatory and respond to people around her but still be under its influence. Combine it with alcohol and ... well it certainly would put her under this man's control, or put her out entirely, as you see."

I didn't get a chance to reply.

The shattered door, which I'd closed to avoid attracting attention, burst open and Duncan came through like a charging rhinoceros.

Before Zamora or I could react, Sterling rushed Duncan, screaming, "Noooo!" in one long bloodcurdling sound.

A crashing blow from Duncan's huge right hand caught Sterling in the jaw and lifted him off his feet. He hit the coffee table in front of the couch with a crash, flat on his back, his head hanging over the end of the table.

Too late, I fired the Colt. The shot hit Duncan in the chest. He fought it, but slowly fell like a collapsing building.

With a cry, Zamora rushed to Duncan's side. I checked Sterling, although with the awkward angle of his head I knew what I'd find. His neck was broken. Alton Sterling was dead.

Zamora cradled Duncan's head in his lap. "You didn't have to kill him. He was just trying to protect me," he wailed, tears in his eyes. "He was like a child, so devoted."

The shreds of the PlastiCuffs were hanging from Duncan's wrists. He'd ripped them apart with sheer strength. I'd heard of that happening, but never believed it possible. He'd used one of Zamora's silk neckties to make a tourniquet that he tied above the leg wound. The will power it took to come all that way after I shot him in the knee was inconceivable.

As Zamora said, maybe devotion explained Duncan's motive. But why did Sterling react the way he did?

"Maybe he just snapped?" I said, thinking out loud. "He'd lost it anyway. Maybe he was trying to protect LeDoux and Duncan breaking in was one too many threats?"

"What does it matter now?" Zamora said, still cradling Duncan's head as tears ran down his face. "You got what you wanted. Now take that woman and get out."

He took in the two bodies. "I hope it was worth it."

"I still need you to show me the way," I said.

"You don't need me. It's easy from here." He gave me the directions. It did sound easy. "I'm not going with you. Shoot me, too, if you wish. But I'm not going anywhere."

Zamora read me well. My appetite for shooting people wasn't that strong.

We had to leave quickly. As well soundproofed as Eros seemed to be, the gunshot was thunderous, although it would be hard for anyone to pinpoint exactly where it came from.

I went to the bedroom closet looking for something to protect LeDoux when we got outside. The first thing I found was one of Sterling's expensive jackets, a navy blazer. It would have to do.

I got her out of bed and wrapped the jacket around her. We left the suite and took off down the hall, leaving Zamora behind, Duncan's head still in his lap.

Chapter Forty-Six

We found the front door easily enough, with LeDoux leaning on me as she stumbled along, head wobbling loose on her shoulders. I had the feeling that her senses were slowly returning, but she couldn't control her body. It was the third time I'd see her like this.

I opened the door panel Duncan used earlier and peered outside. Although it was still afternoon, the sky was so dark that it might as well be midnight. There were no lights on anywhere that I could see. The power must have gone out. No surprise there. From what I could tell in the darkness, it was unexpectedly calm. The street was flooded but the wind seemed mild, considering.

I looked at my watch. I'd been inside for less than two hours. Had the hurricane passed already? It was hard to believe.

We couldn't stay at Eros, not with one guy in handcuffs, two dead bodies inside, and a drug-addled movie star on my arm. We had to risk going out. Even if this was only the eye of the storm and there was more to come, we still might have time to get to the car and then drive like hell to my house, where we could stay until LeDoux recovered.

I opened the door and we stepped into the street. The Mustang was only a block away but progress was slow because it was hard to keep LeDoux moving. The air seemed ominous and heavy, like a weight pressing against us. It was unnaturally calm, but with a sense of looming violence. Damage from Isabel's wrath was all around us; storefronts battered, glass shattered, and trees uprooted. I saw two crumbled garden walls and one house roof partially torn away. The water came almost to our knees as we splashed down the street.

When we rounded the corner to the street where I parked, the sight stopped me cold. While I was inside Eros, a banyan tree uprooted by the storm fell across the car. The tree trunk crushed the driver and passenger seats and virtually cut the car in half.

We weren't going anywhere in the Mustang.

Chapter Forty-Seven

What now? Through the darkness, the angry black clouds seemed closer and swirling more violently. Mild just a moment ago, now the rain came down so hard that if felt like we were taking a beating.

The wind was already twice as strong as it was when we left Eros and growing stronger every second. I'd made a mistake, maybe a deadly mistake. We did leave Eros during the eye of the hurricane, but it was so late in the eye that Isabel was about to hit us again with her full, deadly fury.

We had to find shelter and find it fast.

We turned away from the ruined Mustang and headed back the way we came. The wind slammed us against a storefront, practically knocking me off my feet. I was on the outside and LeDoux cried out in pain when we she took most of my weight when we smashed against the building. She would have fallen if I hadn't held on to her. From there, it was all I could do to get one foot in front of the other as we made slow progress down the street, clutching at anything I could get my hands on for support against the howling wind.

I don't know how, but I sensed something coming. I looked over my shoulder and jumped to one side just in time to avoid a flying Vespa motor scooter that missed us by inches. It would have killed us both. The hurricane threw it down the street like a child's toy.

With the storefronts all boarded up, I was looking for a place to break into, an unprotected door or a small side window. After a few increasingly desperate moments, I found one, a door on a side street with four small glass panels in the upper half that hadn't been boarded up.

Hanging on to LeDoux while I fought the hurricane wind that tried to rip her out of my grasp, we made it to the door. Holding her close with one arm around her waist, I used the butt of the Python to shatter one of the glass panels and knock out the remaining shards. I reached inside, unlocked the door, and roughly shoved her inside, falling in after her with the last of my strength.

I don't know how long I lay on the floor gasping for breath before I recovered enough strength to get up, push the door closed, and lock it.

We were safe, for now.

Chapter Forty-Eight

It was so dark that I had to use my phone as a flashlight. As I feared, cell service was out. We were in a restaurant. The chairs were neatly arranged upside down on the tables and the front-door and windows were covered by wooden shutters. As I poked around the room, I felt the hurricane shake the one-story building like a doll house. The noise was deafening.

I dragged LeDoux to a corner. She still showed no sign of coming out of her drug-induced torpor. I didn't know what Sterling gave her or how long its effects would last. When she recovered, I didn't want her to wake up in a panic, not knowing where she was or who she was with. I sat beside her on the concrete floor and put my arm around her shoulders so she'd have some human contact if she started to come to her senses.

With a massive crash, the wind blew out the remaining glass panels on the door, shards of glass exploding across the restaurant floor. I picked up LeDoux and carried her to another corner as far away from the shattered door as we could get.

There was nothing to do but ride it out. We huddled in the corner, my arm around her shoulders. When the hurricane passed, I'd find a way to either get her to my place or contact Mike Lieber at The Rock and get her back in her suite. The Rock was the better choice because Lieber could provide transportation, assuming it could get here after the storm. For a moment, I'd forgotten that my Mustang was out of commission, probably for good.

Rain poured in through the broken door. It seemed to be seeping through the foundation, too, plus probably a dozen other leaks in the old building. It wasn't long before we were sitting in six inches of water.

As we sat there in the wet darkness, surrounded by the hurricane's din, I heard a noise that I couldn't identify, a shrill screeching that seemed to come and go. Sometimes I could barely hear it and sometimes it was all I could hear. It was so dark that it was impossible to tell the source of the noise or the direction it came from. I briefly tried the light from my cell phone again, but even with that I couldn't see anything as I flashed it around the restaurant. After a few seconds, I turned it off. I didn't want to use up the battery.

I felt water hit my face. The volume seemed to increase. With so much water all around us I didn't think anything of it until I realized that it came from above. I turned on my cell phone light again and looked up.

Directly above us, the hurricane was tearing the roof off he building! The screeching I heard was the roof peeling away!

I saw a gap of several inches between the top of the wall and the roof. The gap doubled in size in the few seconds I watched. It was at least a foot wide now. The wider the gap, the faster it seemed to grow as the roof ripped off along one whole side of the restaurant.

We were trapped. There was no place to go. I pushed LeDoux deeper into the corner and eased my body on top of hers to protect her as best I could. I put my arms around her in the hope that the wind wouldn't rip us apart.

I didn't know if she could hear or understand me, but I yelled in her ear. "Don't give up! It's not over yet! As long as we're alive, we've got a chance!"

With a final massive scream, the roof peeled off and the hurricane hurled it far away. Hell had come to Cabo San Lucas.

Chapter Forty-Nine

In rubber boots that came to his knees and with his hands on his hips, Valencia stood in the middle of what once was the busiest street in Cabo San Lucas and surveyed the damage.

It would certainly be in the hundreds of millions, he thought, starting with the marina. The damage to all those expensive craft, plus the exaggerated insurance claims by the owners, would make many accountants and lawyers happy for a long time.

But Valencia didn't care about self-absorbed millionaires and their expensive toys. Most of the downtown streets still were flooded. Roofs were torn off and walls were down, though not as many as he feared. According to the reports so far, virtually all of the major resorts came through the hurricane in good shape. Most of the resorts were decent enough to offer empty rooms and even space in their lobbies to shelter those who needed it. Falling trees had knocked down so many power lines that it would be days before power was fully restored. The airport seemed to have suffered most. The roof was off one terminal and a wall was down. Military aircraft might be needed to get the tourists home.

Fortunately cell phone service was working again and Valencia could supervise his men who were scattered around the city helping the recovery effort. The available manpower was proving more than sufficient. Representatives from all levels of law enforcement, plus more than two hundred men from the Mexican army, were involved. Medical teams were coming in from all over the country, in addition to Red Cross workers from Mexico and the United States.

So far, eight deaths were reported, with more than one hundred serious injuries. There would be more as rescue teams sorted through the rubble, of that he was certain. Grim as it was, he knew that Cabo San Lucas was lucky. It could have been much worse.

The real problems would come in restoring transportation, power and water. The major resorts had their own systems for water and the city would have to rely on those for some time, which meant they would be overburdened. The federal government had promised that it would fly in thousands of cases of bottled water, although none had arrived yet.

Politicians of every level put in appearances, too, worthless as always. Fortunately, after a few photographs and media interviews, most of them left to seek publicity elsewhere. Cabo San Lucas – his city – would take care of itself. It always had.

"Jefe! Jefe!"

A young police trainee ran up to Valencia as best he could run in the flooded street. His breathing was labored with the effort of making his way through so much water.

"Lieutenant Espinoza asks that you come, quickly please. There is something you must see."

Valencia knew Espinoza to be a reliable man. If he said that his chief was needed there was a good reason for it.

"Show me," he said. The recruit turned back the way he came and Valencia splashed after him.

They rounded a corner and Valencia saw Espinoza standing by a downed Banyan tree that fell across a parked car, crushing it. The car was almost entirely hidden by the tree's wide-spreading limbs. The veteran lieutenant saw him and waved the chief closer.

And then Valencia saw why he was summoned. It was Cruickshank's Mustang crushed beneath the heavy trunk of the fallen tree.

"Is anyone ...?"

Espinoza answered the question before Valencia finished asking.

"No one was in the car and no one has come back to it. I thought you would want to know immediately."

Cruickshank's car was well-known to the Cabo *policia*, as was his sometimes prickly friendship with Valencia.

The chief began barking orders.

"Contact every man we have in the area. Have them report to me right here. Anyone who takes longer than five minutes will spend the rest of their careers directing traffic."

While Valencia waited for his men to assemble, he paced back and forth, not even noticing the deep water. He punched in Cruickshank's cell but it went directly to message.

He summoned the trainee who delivered Espinoza's message and motioned to a nearby *policia* SUV. "Take that vehicle and go to this address." He wrote down Cruickshank's address in the small notebook he carried with him, tore off the page and handed it to the youngster. "You will see if anyone is there, especially the man named Ethan Cruickshank. Whatever you find, even if it's nothing, call me immediately."

"But *jefe*, that SUV is assigned to Sergeant Gomez," the trainee protested. "He won't like it if...."

"I don't care if it is assigned to God," snapped Valencia. "Do what I tell you!"

Something was wrong, terribly wrong. Why was Cruickshank downtown during the hurricane? Where had he gone? Valencia knew how much the American loved the Mustang. Why did he leave it out in the open when he knew the storm was coming?

His men were assembled. No one dared to be late. They knew that the chief didn't make idle threats.

"Whatever you were doing you will stop immediately. You will fan out from this spot in all directions. Lieutenant Espinoza will coordinate your movements. You will enter every building, you will go down every alley, and you will sift through every bit of rubble. If you need help for any reason, contact me and I will see that you get it. You are looking for an American named Ethan Cruickshank. Most of you know what he looks like. Ask if you do not. Now go!"

One man lingered, unsure of himself and what he was about to ask.

"*Jefe*, what about our duties? We were aiding in ...."

"I don't care what you *were* doing. I have told you what you *will* do and if you don't start this second I will drown you in the filthy water at your feet! Go!"

Valencia remembered Cruickshank's inquiry about Eros and issued one more order.

"Sergeant Gomez!"

The overweight sergeant huffed forward, the water sloshing at his knees.

"Yes, *Jefe*."

"Sergeant, I ordered your vehicle used for another purpose. I want you to go to a place called Eros. Do you know where it is?" When Gomez said that he had never heard of it, Valencia gave him directions. "You will find a man named Zamora. If they say he is not there, you will enter and make *sure* he is not there. If he is there you will ask about the American Ethan Cruickshank. Has he seen him? If so, when and what happened? Find out everything you can and report back to me before you leave Eros."

With his men gone, Valencia joined the search.

Chapter Fifty

Twenty minutes later, Valencia received a call.

"*Jefe*, please come quickly. We have found him. There is one other, too."

Valencia hurried to the address, which he knew to be a small nondescript restaurant that offered the usual Cabo tourist fare: indifferent seafood, weak margaritas, and buckets of iced beer for ten dollars.

The patrolman who called said that the only way to get in was through a side door damaged by the hurricane. Following directions, Valencia passed through the open door, although he could easily have stepped over what remained of one wall. The roof was torn away, too. No doubt the building would be reckoned a total loss. Another one just as badly built would take its place.

It was light enough outside, but with the front of the restaurant shuttered, it was dim inside. It took a moment for Valencia's eyes to adjust. When they did, he saw two men clawing at the floor in one corner.

When he stepped closer he saw Cruickshank half buried under cinder block rubble from the wall, his face covered in dried blood.

Valencia knelt down beside the body, feeling for a pulse.

"Is he ...?"

"He is still alive," one patrolman said. "So is the other one. We don't know how badly they are injured."

It was only then that Valencia saw a second body beneath Cruickshank. It was the actress. The detective had his arms around her. It appeared that he had deliberately absorbed the brunt of the falling rubble with his own body. Although unconscious, she had no obvious injuries.

Valencia called for an ambulance and began to help clear away the rubble without disturbing the bodies beneath, analyzing the scene as he worked.

Cruickshank was armed, with a Colt Python in a shoulder holster. One did not carry a weapon like that without intent. Knowing Cruickshank's habits, Valencia found a second weapon in an ankle holster. So the detective was expecting trouble, or at least he was prepared for it.

As the debris slowly cleared, the situation became more unusual. The actress was wearing a man's dark blue blazer over an expensive satin gown. Hardly hurricane wear.

Where were they going? Or, perhaps more important, where had they been?

Given the actress' unusual attire and Cruickshank's recent inquiry, Eros seemed like a strong possibility, although Valencia knew enough about Cruickshank's taste in women to doubt that they had gone there for the usual reasons.

When Sergeant Gomez called from Eros, he reported that no one could find Alonzo Zamora, which had everyone on the staff worried because Zamora lived on site and was known to be there when the hurricane struck. Apparently his personal aide, a man the rest of the staff knew only as Duncan, was also missing.

The ambulance arrived and Cruickshank and the actresses were carefully loaded into it, to be taken to the already overcrowded hospital.

"How does it look?" Valencia asked the paramedic.

"It is impossible for me to say," he replied as he secured both patients inside the ambulance. "It probably depends on if he has internal injuries, I think."

Valencia called the hospital chief of staff to explain that these patients should receive particularly attentive care. The overworked and exhausted physician said that he would look into it personally. It probably was the tenth time he said that today.

Chapter Fifty-One

"Two broken ribs, a fractured skull, a chipped vertebra, and a broken ankle; yet you say he will be all right?"

"Yes, I do. When he grows old, he probably will have some arthritis issues at the points of injury, but, yes, he if there are no complications he should be fine. It is remarkable. The man must have a head like a rock."

"You have no idea how true that is."

I tried to say something to interrupt the conversation that seemed to be floating somewhere above me, but all that came out was a feeble, dry croak.

Something was put in my mouth, at the corner.

"Here, try this."

I reflexively sucked on it and the most delicious thing I ever tasted cascaded into my mouth from what I now recognized was a hooked tube.

I went back for seconds and was about to try for a third when the tube was removed. I was so disappointed that I felt like crying.

"Not too much all at once. What were you trying to say?"

"I can hear you," I said, my voice still a hoarse whisper. "It's not polite to talk about me like I'm not here."

"Trust me," Valencia said, "for a long time you were not."

* * *

I was still in the hospital when Odermeyer entered the room, looking a lot better than the last time I saw him.

Pulling up a chair beside the bed, he put a small backpack on the floor beside it. He explained that he'd come once before, but I was so out of it that I made no sense.

"Who's Dina?" he asked. "You kept talking to her, though I couldn't understand most of it."

"Someone I used to know," I said. That part of the conversation wasn't going any further.

"I wanted to let you know that we wrap it up here tomorrow," he said. "It's earlier than we planned, but what's left we can take care of back home. Everybody's glad to get out."

"How's Rio?"

"You mean she hasn't come to see you?"

When I said no, he responded with an explosive sigh.

"I guess I'm not surprised, considering that all you did was save her life. Hell, she wasn't even hurt except a few bruises. If what hit you had hit her, she'd be dead."

I told him I wasn't surprised either, mostly because I wasn't.

So there we were; two not surprised guys.

He lifted the backpack from the floor, put it on his lap, opened it, rummaged, and handed me a white envelope.

"Here's your check. The doc says you'll be discharged in a couple of days. We paid you up to that point, plus another week, and the studio will take care of your medical bills for as long as you need treatment."

"Miscellaneous expenses," I said.

"You sure are."

"What about Sterling?" I knew what the official line was, but I wanted to hear details.

"So far they've managed to cover it all up as far as I can tell," he said. "I don't know everything myself. Frankly, I don't want to. It's remarkable really. They'd never pull that off back home."

"Or maybe they do it all the time and they're so good at it that nobody knows," I said

"Good point," he admitted. "Anyway, the story is that Sterling's body was found someplace outside after the hurricane. Broken neck. Something probably hit him. Turned out he was having some problems in his private life and things were a helluva mess. The guy turned out to be a nutcase. It's probably better for his reputation that he's dead."

I knew that Valencia colluded on the business with Sterling. We had talked about it a couple of days earlier. Sterling was obsessed with LeDoux, probably had been for years, though he hid it well until the last. The man devoted everything to her. What he wanted to get out of it was anybody's guess. Love? Admiration? Who knows? When he figured out that she was going to dump him he lost it. What did he plan to do with her? That was another unknown. People who go off the deep end rarely make sense. I know. I've been there. Looking for logic is a fool's errand.

With all of Cabo's problems after the hurricane, Valencia wanted this one to go away and helped make it happen. It was better for everybody. I never asked what happened to Zamora. Maybe he didn't know. Maybe he did. I didn't particularly care. And Duncan? Nobody knew anything. Duncan who? It was as if he never existed.

"Look, I'm sure Rio wanted to come see you," Odermeyer said. "She just doesn't handle stuff like this very well. Hospitals depress her."

"They don't do a lot for me either," I said. "Besides, it really doesn't matter."

"What do you mean?"

It was hard to explain, but I gave it a try.

"There *were* times when I felt sorry for her and wished that I liked her better, but I'm glad I didn't."

"Why is that?"

"She'll always be the way she is," I said. "And everybody else will pay for it."

About the Author

Robert Wisehart is the author of three other novels about the adventures of private detective Ethan Cruickshank. They are *Cabo*, *Cabo Revenge*, and *Cabo Sunset*. He also has written three historical novels about the tumultuous life and career of American soldier-statesman Sam Houston: *Born for the Storm*, *The Rising*, and *The Lion at Bay*.

A native of Indianapolis, Indiana, Wisehart is a former award-winning journalist who worked as a reporter and columnist for newspapers in Florida, North Carolina, Louisiana and California. His work has appeared in more than thirty magazines and 200 newspapers. He has written speeches, ghosted books and routinely eaten too much and attempted to regurgitate the experience in words as a restaurant critic. Moving often and traveling wisely, Wisehart lives with his wife, Dana, in

Santa Fe, New Mexico, where he works on his next novel and plays enthusiastic tennis.

To Our Readers

Black Kettle Books is a collaborative publisher, proud to work in partnership with outstanding authors to bring inventive and engaging works – both fiction and nonfiction, new and previously overlooked – to a wider audience. Ask for Black Kettle Books in select bookstores and other fine retailers.

blackkettlebooks@gmail.com

Made in the USA
Lexington, KY
19 March 2015